I0891275

The Revisionist
A Case in Documents

Tobias Roberts

THE REVISIONIST

A CASE IN DOCUMENTS

DALKEY ARCHIVE PRESS
Dallas / Dublin

First Dalkey Archive edition, 2020

ISBN: 978-1-62897-321-1
CIP Data forthcoming

www.dalkeyarchive.com
Dallas / Dublin

Printed on permanent/durable acid-free paper.

For Rebecca

My one true constant

A Book in shape but, really, pure crude fact
Secreted from man's life when hearts beat hard . . .
(. . .)
                    . . . Learn one lesson hence
Of many which whatever lives should teach:
This lesson, that our human speech is naught,
Our human testimony false, our fame
And human estimation words and wind.
(. . .)
But Art, —wherein man nowise speaks to men,
Only to mankind, —Art may tell a truth
Obliquely, do the thing shall breed the thought,
Nor wrong the thought, missing the mediate word.

The Ring and the Book
Robert Browning

BOOK TWO

Table of Documents

BOOK ONE

Acknowledgements

In an enterprise as difficult to complete as a novel, the task could not be done (at least in my case) without the invaluable help of family, friends and colleagues. First, I wish to thank my tireless editor, Jacob Miller, for his excellent suggestions and ideas arising from his constant critical and creative scrutiny which led to seeing this novel through to completion. Secondly, I want to thank my wife, Rebecca, for her encouragement during the three years I worked on this book. I wish to thank my colleagues in my writing group for their input and ideas as the novel developed and matured over the years.

One separate group of friends I especially wish to thank are Hayden Miller, Ekatrina Svetova and Karen Grey Ruelle. Without their artistic efforts on my behalf, this work would have been incomplete. Mr. Hayden Miller was responsible for Abram's Superman Comic Book. Ms. Svetova was responsible for the drawing of Abram Weiss by his sister, Sara, the magic show poster and coordinating all graphics for this project. Finally, Ms. Ruelle was responsible for the drawings that go with Sara Himmelfarb's children story, *Prouty Spaniel Takes a Walk.*

BOOK THREE

BOOK FOUR

Preface

Initially, I planned to begin this work with a discussion of the concept of Logokinesis Mania, a term coined by my father-in-law, Dr. Zachary Weiss. I would have shown how Dr. Weiss had a patient, whom my father-in-law named J, who thought he could alter printed text physically through will power. Then my narrative was to show how this case led me to re-examine aspects of my life, my family, and others closest to me. But, with experience, I came to feel such a work would only create an illusion for the reader of narrative certainty, a certainty I now no longer possess.

I gave up my efforts to tell this story as a novel or a scientific tract. Now instead of throwing out all the documents, which I seriously considered doing for some time, I give the reader two books containing the raw data of the case along with my diary entries (which at the time arose largely over concerns about my wife's health), as well as later documents relevant to the story of The Revisionist. Some documents here have been edited to make the facts unfold smoothly, while many others, most, I haven't touched. Readers might call me lazy for not assuming the expected authority in telling this story, but as I have lost belief in the idea of an authoritative narrative, let them find the certainty I could not.

According to medieval Kabbalists, the Torah could have 600,000 possible interpretations (one interpretation each for the 600,000 children of Israel present with Moses at Mount Sinai) and its very letters could change their order of sequence to correspond to the condition of the world at the time they were being read. The ancients knew how mutable a text was. As Solomon said, "Everything under the sun has been done and will be done again."

And yet that quest to understand how we seek the immutable in what is mutable continues.

Isaac Himmelfarb
December 20, 2018

BOOK ONE

1.
Family Trees for the Himmelfarb and Weiss Families

The Himmelfarbs

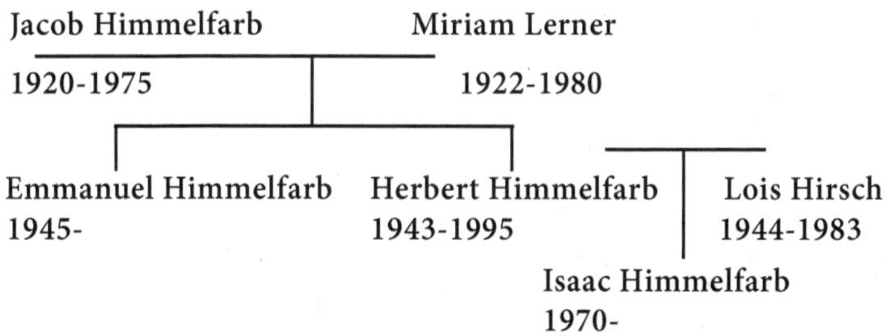

The Weisses

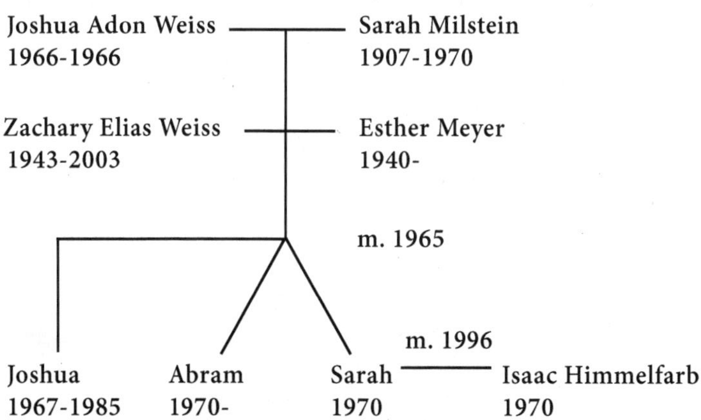

2.
"Big Wig Shrink's Career Shrinks"

New York Post, October 12, 2007
By Betty Minor

We hear that Dr. Zachary Weiss, a well known psychotherapist and writer who has very privately been the headshrinker to many well-heeled celebrities, has been himself the subject of weird rumors about seeing patients with psychokinetic skills ever since reducing his practice last spring.

Psychokinesis is the out-there theory that it's possible for the human brain physically to affect material objects. Many respectable scientists dismiss the idea as New Age hooey. Others have argued that tests have shown the brain might be more powerful than anyone has guessed before.

Adding to this uproar over Psychokinesis is the accusation that the theory is nothing more than a get-rich-quick scam peddled by New Age con artists to a gullible public.

There've been stories going around Dr. Weiss's fellow headshrinkers that he was seeing patients who said they could really do this. One even claimed he was able physically to change printed words by brain power alone. We hear that when Dr. Weiss tried to convince colleagues of the truth of his patients' claims, they thought he'd gone nuts. A psych test was given at Colombia, but the results were kept under wraps. They must have been bad for the good doctor.

None of Dr. Weiss's doctor friends wanted to talk about the test. Obviously, they were afraid of looking like dummies if they told anyone outside their charmed circle what one of their big-shot members was willing to swallow from his nutso patients. No wonder Dr. Weiss seems ready to put his shingle into storage for the duration.

3.
Obituary, The New York Times

March 20, 2018

Zachary Elias Weiss, 60, Noted Clinical Psychiatrist, Author; Specialized in Abnormal Psychology
Ivor Wissenschaft

Zachary Elias Weiss, 60, psychiatrist and author of many books and articles on abnormal psychology, died March 20 at Memorial Sloan-Kettering Hospital. Dr. Weiss was known for his wide range of interests such as exploring the psychological roots behind the creative impulse in the arts, examining the role played by ideas as forces driving historical events and, when young, protested against the Vietnam War.

Trained in psychiatric medicine at Harvard Medical School, he interned at the Cornell Medical Center-New York Hospital in White Plains, NY, where he developed his interest in abnormal psychology especially in cases of delusional obsession, which would serve as the basis for his monograph on the subject, *Obsession and Mania* (1985), a work hailed by critics as a major contribution to the field of psychology. Other major works include *Manic Depressions: Creative Destruction* (1988), *Obsession: A Study in Psychological Displacement* (1992), *Those Creative Madmen*, (1995) a study of artists and writers who used their obsessions to creative ends, which many felt was his best work, *The Structure of Belief* (1998), and his last major work, *The Persistence of an Idea: The Key to Mania* (2003).

After a three-year residency at New York Hospital in White Plains, Dr. Weiss entered into private practice. Born in Queens, New York City on August 12, 1957, to Joshua and Sara Weiss, he later settled in Westport, Connecticut in 1984. After his internship in New York, he worked from 1984 until he all but closed his practice in 2007, after the Revisionist Case.

A patient persuaded Dr. Weiss he had the ability to alter physically printed text mentally. When colleagues failed to be persuaded of his patient's fantastic claim, Dr. Weiss stopped accepting new patients, apparently after concerns about his own mental health were raised.

After this, Dr. Weiss was virtually retired. In his final years, the only colleague with whom Dr. Weiss kept in close contact and continued to share his Connecticut office was his son-in-law, Dr. Isaac Himmelfarb, a child psychologist. The cause of death was stomach cancer.

His eldest son, Joshua, died in a car accident in 1989.

Dr. Weiss is survived by his wife Esther, his son Abram, and his daughter, Sara.

4.
The Diary of Isaac Himmelfarb

March 20, 2018

Sara. Sweet Sara, she's lost so much, our child, her brother, Joshua, Abram and now her father, Zach. It was hard enough for Sara, for the both of us, to watch her father slowly die. Here I am, supposed to be a psychiatrist like Zach was, and yet I find myself unable to mitigate or stop his daughter and my wife's slide into a deeper depression.

The gradual accumulation of her problems over the years: her fear of her father's growing obsession with his patient, Pierce—talking constantly of his case, the potential malleability of language, meaning, communication. She would try to change the topic at the dinner table, but as his obsession grew, so did Zach's annoyance at interruptions.

All in the midst of Zach's growing obsession, faced with which I, as a psychiatric professional and colleague, could not help being torn by equal parts of intrigue and skepticism, I neglected my wife—fine damn professional I am! I responded inadequately to her anxieties about her pregnancy and later, shouldn't there have been some way I could have been there more for her after her miscarriage? Well, screw me!

Sara's problems, her behavior at the *Shiva*, made clear how far advanced her depression was. I had to deal with the caterers, cover all the mirrors, attend to the guests. Esther, Sara's mom—the widow—should have done all the arrangements but, with her Alzheimer's, I'm not sure she even grasps that Zach is dead, much less buried. Meantime, Sara lost our baby, had her miscarriage, just two weeks before losing her father, Zach.

After the funeral, Sara was like a zombie during the *Shiva* visits, barely acknowledging anyone who came. Everyone was sympathetic. She had, after all, lost her baby and then her dad. But, damn! it was as if she didn't notice or hear a word anyone uttered to her.

Screw it! She was half-way through her pregnancy and obsessing about fixing up a cute nursery—the room for the baby, making me spend hours putting together the crib which, not being mechanically inclined, took me forever to work on and still was not finished, then, with no warning, the baby was gone, lost, and Sara's father, at almost the exact same time, was clearly being taken away by cancer, damn disease.

Six years ago, that's when it first appeared, just after that awful Revisionist Case crippled his practice. To think that after enormous success as a renowned psychiatrist for more than thirty years, it took only one patient and a mutated cellular growth to demolish decades of great work. Fuck! A patient challenging the potential for altering reality in print coinciding with Zach's body altering the stability of his cellular composition would have been enough to drive anyone to questions no one wants to face. Is it possible Zach's patient, Pierce, somehow triggered his cancer as well?

The few times Zach spoke to me about the Revisionist Case, he'd say things like: "How can I go on if someone can make me see things changing as easily as flipping a switch on or off? If one's perception of fixity is as easily undermined as my revisionist showed, how can I trust anything I see? What if what we all think we see is really vulnerable to some abstract malleability, even something like printed text, which ought to be fixed and permanent, never in flux and changing?"

Just two weeks before Zach died, when Sara had her miscarriage and I was grieving with her, Zach came into our perfect nursery one night with the crib I'd incompletely assembled, which now would remain empty, and staring at the crib Zach muttered: "Why not? Why not just language on a page—couldn't life itself be vulnerable? couldn't precisely the same abstract malleability be what took my grandchild from us?"

There was nothing to say to my father-in-law when Zach uttered such remarks, as on that night when he muttered his wild words then suddenly left the nursery. The next two weeks, Zach was in a complete fog while dear Sara nursed her wounds from our lost child—the house was grim and maybe, though I hate like hell to write it down here, it was almost a relief when Zach finally lost his battle with cancer.

Now the pain-in-the-butt task of cleaning up will begin. I start getting sick every time I go into Zach's office next door and see the boxes piled up, one on top of another, all full of his notes, documents, drafts, doodles. I haven't even gotten my practice really going and now I have to deal with this. But, it has to be done. The good news is Zach saved everything and, as executor of his estate, he told me I would have complete discretion as to how to dispose of his papers.

5.
Zach's Son Abram's Superman Comic

1982

Howdy Superman
Terraman-
You escaped again-
So what if I did Lawman?
You'll have to face the consequences. Give up now.
No way-You don't have a chance-
Take this!
Superman felt weak but his mind was still strong so he thought of getting back his powers until ...
1

WHAT? AHHH—
I've decided your Kryptonite raygun cannot hurt me. Like my heatvision Terraman?
Please, Superman, Take pity on me and meet my sidekick, 20th Century Billy the Kid.
Who?
Billy Anders!? What did Terraman do to you? By the way, I decided Krypto-rays don't bother me—
Superman was eventually able to break Terraman's spell over Billy but, meantime, Terraman crawled into a strange building...
2

What's this? Lead Doors! I can't see through lead but maybe if I concentrate very hard—
Aha! There you are Terraman. I've got a one-way ticket for you to the exile dimension.
COMING SUPER ATTRACTIONS
IN THE DECEMBER ACTION COMICS
SUPERMAN BECOMES
"THE MOST DANGEROUS MAN ON EARTH!"
PLUS ALSO IN JANUARY LOOK FOR ACTION IN "THE HUMAN TARGET!"
3

6.
Zachary Weiss's note on New Patient Pierce, Hereinafter ref'd to as J

J born and raised in Venice, California—Spoke fondly of childhood home on Esperanza Drive, nice yard to play in, with a picket fence like in old Andy Hardy movies J was fond of on TV. Noted his preference for viewing idealized family situations unlike his own with absent dad, preoccupied mom—J spoke of that yard incessantly—how he played make-believe war games and sci-fi stories in which he could let his imagination run wild and always emerge the hero.

J's parents divorced in his last year of high school. His father recently deceased. Mother remarried, living in Boston. J took divorce badly—kept in touch with neither parent.

J reluctantly revealed his childhood home, the house and yard, was seized recently by the state under eminent domain and demolished to make way for freeway extension. J became quite agitated as he disclosed that he recently went to where his family's house had been and sat for hours by the side of the highway, staring at a broad stretch of white picket fence half-buried in the mud by an exit ramp to the new highway.

Given his obvious anxiety over the recent death of his father and the loss of his childhood home, I prescribed a short-term regime of Xanax to help settle his nerves. T. Wolfe right in J's case, he really couldn't go home again.

7.
Notes from *The Revisionist: A Case of Logokinesis Mania*

Dr. Zachary Weiss

"Kafka," J muttered as he sank back into his chair, lacing his fingers together and resting them on his lap, and stared at the wall of books in my office.

"Brilliant writer, of course, but what about him?" I knew this new patient, Pierce, worked in publishing and so would naturally be drawn to scrutinize my library, but also felt he was avoiding direct eye contact.

"It all began with Franz Kafka. I've always admired his work, especially the *Metamorphosis*. Well, you recall his great opening line?"

I nodded, and waited for him to continue.

"'After a restless night, Gregor Samsa awoke to discover he had been transformed into a giant bug,'" J recited, then asked me an unusual question. "Hasn't it ever bothered you, perhaps even gnawed at you, that Kafka never mentioned what kind of bug? Gregor Samsa had been changed into some sort of insect—fine! But, what sort? Roach? Beetle? What?"

J was clearly agitated as I pondered the best response I could offer him. In the end, I went for simplicity, "No, to be honest, I never truly thought at length as to what type of insect exactly, but you raise a legitimate literary question."

"Well, for me, shortly after my father first became ill, even though I was always busy at work editing books, meeting with authors and the like, this question kept running through my mind: What kind of insect, exactly, had Gregor Samsa been changed into? I thought about it at lunch, as I walked on the sidewalk or rode the subway or at home, at night it nagged at me when I ate dinner alone. Then, right after my father died, it happened." J stopped speaking abruptly, then finally turned from looking at my bookcase to face me.

"And, what was that?"

"What?"

"What happened after your father passed away?"

"First, I had this really strange dream that I had become a dung beetle and was rolling a huge ball of shit up to heaven. This ball was as large as the earth and a voice kept telling me, 'You must place this near the sun.' When I did so, the ball began to seethe like it was full of unformed life and began changing colors like some psychedelic kaleidoscope. That's when I awoke, bathed in sweat."

"Fascinating," I said.

"Worse was to come. The dream upset me so much, I suddenly got out of bed and hurried over to my bookshelf and grabbed my copy of the *Metamorphosis*. As I was about to open the book, a sudden wave of fear swept over me. For a minute, I just stood there trembling. Finally, I opened the book to the first page and read the first line. I then saw that it read: "After a restless night, Gregor Samsa awoke to discover he had been transformed into a giant dung beetle." I couldn't believe it. Was I still dreaming? I turned and looked at my bed, half expecting to see myself still in it, but my bed was empty and so I turned my eyes back to the first page of the book in my hands. I looked at Kafka's first sentence again and found it now read: "After a restless night, Gregor Samsa awoke to discover he had been transformed into an exhausted giant dung beetle."

"Well, that isn't too surprising actually. Often when I read a book and I'm tired, I can nod off and then wake up, but being still half-asleep, I can look at what I was reading and the text can appear changed, with words on the page not as I'd remembered reading before. Maybe something like that happened to you since you said you had just awoken after that unusual dream. It appeared the Kafka text had changed because you weren't fully awake yet."

J frowned and raised his voice. "No, no, no! I was fully awake!"

"It was just a thought. I understand now that you were fully awake. Would you mind if we move in another direction for a moment?"

"Whatever—you're the doc."

"I was just wondering: might you tell me a bit about your father?"

"Like what?"

"How about, for starters, was he a fan of literature, an avid reader and, if so, had you ever spoken with him of Kafka's work?"

"Dad, interested in literature? That's a goddamn laugh. My old man sold textbooks in bulk to primary schools and secondary schools, but he couldn't care less what was in them. All he cared about was bulk sales to school districts and he only ever got excited when he landed a state contract covering several school districts. Then he'd go on about what a great commission he was going to get from his company. 'Just give a good line about how superior our textbooks are, shake their hand, look them in the eye and tell a funny story. That's all there's to it,' he'd say. Once I asked him if he'd ever read any of the textbooks he sold, and he just shook his head, 'Nah, sometimes I fan through the books and see how many glossy illustrations they have. Look, I know how to BS the principal or the state board about how the kids will love our books, the illustrations are eye-catching and will help the kids learn.' Then Dad would lean in and whisper to me, 'In fact, I don't know what crap, if any, the kids learn from these books but, man, that line really helps me move inventory.' Work aside, my dad mostly drank beer and watched sports. As for him talking to me about Kafka—hell, he couldn't have told you the difference between Kafka and a hole in the wall."

"How about after you ended up working as an editor—did you speak with him about literature at all then?"

"You don't get it—we never spoke about literature. Hell, come to think of it, a few times I did try to share my excitement after I started working as an editor, but he pretty much told me he thought literature and editing was work for women and 'faggots'. All he ever asked about my work was to do with income and benefits, certainly not the content or character of the manuscripts I was working on. No, my dad didn't give a shit for literature of any kind."

"Isn't it curious that you used the word 'shit' in connection with both your father and literature just now?"

"What are you saying?"

"Well, you tell me: do you think there might be a connection between your father and your dream about the dung beetle and you?"

J started squirming in his chair and sunk his face into his hands. When he looked up at me, he was frowning again. Softly, but firmly, he said, "No! My old man had nothing to do with that damn dream and what happened to the text of the Kafka translation. You either don't get it or haven't been listening—the first line of *The Metamorphosis* had actually changed from 'bug to 'dung beetle', and then again changed to add that the dung beetle was 'exhausted.'"

J's statement challenged my initial diagnosis of the issues he presented. "I'd like to understand. It's just a bit complex. So let me see if I've got this right now: you mean you believe your dream had mentally re-edited the physical text or you thought you actually read those differing translations in the same book that night?"

J glared at me. With a sharp wave of his right hand, he shouted, "No, no, no! You don't get it at all! Look—I told you, right after my dad died, *IT* happened, and you asked me what happened and now I've told you. What I told you is exactly what happened. I had that dream and then observed, for the first time, that my mind—the dream, whatever—could somehow actually change the actual printed words in a book."

"So, what you're telling me is that you believe you somehow

have the capacity to alter physical text in a book through some part of your mind or psyche?"

"In a nutshell, yes, that's it. I not only believe I have this capacity; I know I do!"

8.
Sara's Drawing of Abram

9.
The Diary of Isaac Himmelfarb

June 4, 2018

Maybe Zach had been too much of a skeptic all his life, but when Pierce approached him, Pierce somehow tapped into a strongly suppressed desire on Zach's part to believe wholeheartedly in something with metaphysical dimensions. Reading over his notes written when he was first treating J, it all seems quite ordinary, routine psychoanalytic dialogue to delve deeper—but did Zach, in the end, delve too deep?

Meantime, I'm trying to open up my wife Sara's depression, which feels like trying to open a door to a Manhattan apartment, lined with so many locks, needing so many keys. Perhaps the most obvious key is the loss of our baby, which she was carrying, then another obvious key to be turned is the death of her father, after all Zach's years of quiet sadness subsequent to retiring in disgrace. Additional keys might be found in the absence of both her brothers at the funeral. Her eldest brother, Joshua, already long deceased, of course, could not magically appear, but what of Abram? Had my wife, Sara, been holding out hopes that Abram might make it to Zach's funeral?

Sara's twin brother, Abram, disappeared during college, before even finishing his freshman year. I always suspected that he might be in some institution. I felt Zach knew; but neither Sara nor I could get much out of him. Zach was silent about Abram.

It was my mom and dad who unintentionally introduced me to Abram in 1992, sometime in July, after bedtime. It was also then that I first met and spoke with Sara. I was eight years old, as were Abram and Sara. I was already in bed, but was woken when I heard my dad shouting. Dad was complaining that a strange kid kept sitting on our lawn after dark. Mom thought that Dad should go out again and find out why the boy continued to do so even after Dad had chased him away before, but that night I volunteered to go speak with the boy sitting on our lawn in the dark.

Coming up to Abram, who remained seated on the grass, I introduced myself and asked him his name. Abram looked at me with faraway eyes and said his parents called him Abram but he had always wanted a name like Mezentius. I asked him: Why Mezentius?

Abram said that he wanted to change his name because all great magicians had made-up names, like Harry Houdini, who was born Erich Weiss. (Interestingly, looking back on it today through the lens of both an adult and a psychoanalyst, I wonder if Abram was drawn to the greatest escape artist of all time because Houdini was both Jewish and also originally named Weiss. Did Zach's son, Abram, want to escape both his heritage and his name?)

At that point, Sara came out of her house in her pajamas and robe and crossed over to my backyard. Coming toward us, illuminated by the light behind her, she looked like one of those fairies out of *A Midsummer Night's Dream*, not of this world.

Abram told his sister that it was okay, he'd be coming home soon. He told Sara that I was his new friend and that we all should be friends. His comment seemed odd as we had only just met. Sara smiled and said that'd be nice.

With all of us seated, I recall asking Abram why he wanted to be a magician. Abram was hesitant to respond; then, he let out that he really wanted to be Superman. I laughed, insisting Superman wasn't real. Sara said that if anyone could do it someday, it'd be Abram. Through magic, Abram said, there must be a way he could make himself Superman. If he closed his eyes and thought really hard about the way he wanted things, he knew he could change the world. Even at the age of eight, as a little boy, Abram's statement made a great impression on me, both startling me and scaring me slightly when he claimed he could change things when he read comic books.

When I doubted Abram's ability, Sara butted in, leaning forward and fiercely nodding her head, saying her brother really could change things. Then Abram explained how he read the first few pages of his Superman comic and then the last few pages and then he closed his eyes and imagined the rest showing how the story reached that last page. He saw each cartoon box in his head and he told the story the way he wanted to tell it.

Occasionally, Sara stroked his shoulders while he was speaking. Clearly, Sara loved her brother Abram deeply. I wonder now if that night, that moment, that observation was when I first began thinking it would be great if Sara could love me that deeply.

Abram said that he'd later see his "thought stories" and the comics were sometimes close to each other. Sometimes they weren't. (Indeed, Abram's Superman comics—at the top of the first box I opened in Zach's office today, with Abram's own drawings inserted in between, telling the story the way he wanted it told—showed Abram changing the rules about Superman's vulnerabilities. What was remarkable was that he was retelling the story by having Superman eliminate anything that could stop him through will power. It was almost identical to J's obsession, though Pierce first demonstrated it with Kafka rather than a comic book.)

What of the revised story line in Abram's comic book that allowed Superman to be able to see through lead? What of J's revision of Kafka's *Metamorphosis*? Maybe I should check out Zach's files regarding J's childhood. Thinking back to this fantasy of Abram's, I can see how J and Abram might have found their ideas compatible. And maybe it's not so aberrant a desire—don't all of us wrestle with longings to change different things from how they are to how we'd like them to be?

Indeed, if I had the power to flip a mental switch and have

that damn crib, which took me so long to assemble not even completely, be occupied with Sara's and my living baby, rather than the grim reality of its emptiness, its vacancy—our loss, the death we must now live with each day—wouldn't I flip that switch as fast as I could? Wouldn't I line up next to J to gain access to that switch, just as Zach so likely was tempted to?

10.
Notes from *The Revisionist: A Case of Logokinesis Mania*

Dr. Zachary Weiss

In our early sessions after I first met with J, he seemed to shy away from again speaking directly about his conviction that he could physically alter texts on a page with his mind or psyche, perhaps not yet trusting me enough due to my initial response in our first meeting when he tried to explain his conviction as to his, at first blush, seemingly delusional capacity. Instead, over the next sessions we dedicated time to discussing J's childhood. He described his mother as a superficial vamp, more interested in older men, clothes and makeup than raising him.

"Did your mother have any interest in art or literature?"

"No, not really, she worked as a salesperson in a costume jewelry store; they didn't even sell real gems, just cut glass or fake diamonds made of cubic zirconium. She did have a talent, though, for finding the right sort of pieces a woman would look good in. Like my dad, she was most excited by selling things to people and using her charm to persuade them to purchase the most expensive necklaces, bracelets and earrings. Often the customer would be accompanied by an older gentleman and Mom knew how to play the old man so he would spend more than he intended on his 'lady love.'

"Like Dad, she'd drop a pearl of wisdom, 'Sonny, guys are

interested in one thing from women. If I can bat my eyes and get them to imagine themselves with me, I can get them to buy stuff for their girlfriends like they were a substitute for me.'"

I concluded that J's parents actually complemented each other. Each was interested only in the outward appearance of things. Neither of them had any interest in exploring any kind of inner depths within themselves or others, much less their son.

Over the next sessions, it rapidly became apparent to me that J had grown up disappointed by his parents and felt they lived in their own worlds, which he didn't respect and where he played only a minor role.

That J's father was frequently away from home, traveling to sell his school textbooks for private and public schools up and down the Northeastern U.S., left J with an unsatisfying home life which, in the absence of any real sense of family, stimulated J's imagination intensely as a means of escaping his actual situation. His interest in books and literature, I concluded, was J's way of trying to alter an unacceptable reality.

"The single time Dad stayed at home for longer than normal was when the latest edition of one of the standard eighth-grade level science textbooks he was to book orders for had a series of typos and, even more seriously, had omitted one key chapter. The whole printing had to be thrown out and a corrected version of the new edition produced. Dad was on the phone constantly talking to the publisher, making sure a corrected version of the textbook was being printed. When I asked him if this meant he actually had to read the textbook in question, he patted my head affectionately and smiled, 'Hell no, I just have to stay on top of the publisher so he will keep holding his proofreaders' feet to the fire to make sure the text is correct this time. I don't want to ruin my reputation by pushing shoddy crap on my customers. That's a first-class trip to eventual unemployment.'"

This gave me some insight into the birth of J's fascination with editing. The need to improve and correct texts had kept J's father at home when he was still a little boy and so, it perhaps followed that in J's formative years and young mind, editing might have been a means of keeping his father closer to him.

But even the young J soon learned editing mistakes would only be a temporary solution to his dilemma: how to get closer to his father. I inferred that J kept hoping during this time that some other incident of an editing mistake in a print run of textbooks would occur, such that father and son might have a genuine heart-to-heart conversation about what mattered to J.

But J reported that, "Once the problem with the eighth-grade science textbooks had been cleared up and no further ones occurred, my dad resumed his long road trips filling book orders. Yeah, he'd keep in touch by phone, asking how school was going and that sort of thing. But I quickly learned that he wanted one-word answers to his questions. If I tried to go into detail, he'd say he had to get off the phone because he was expecting an important call."

J shared with me that he spent almost all of his free time in the high school library, avoiding all social activity with his peers and inhaling one book after another, glued to his chair, reading. Over time, J admitted that he developed the habit of secretly crossing out words in the library books he was reading and scribbling his own words over the printed text he had crossed out. He admitted he wasn't quite certain what motivated him to edit those books in the school library, but he reported that it brought him an odd comfort and a peculiar sense of hope each time he found what he felt was a mistake in the printed text.

However, sadly for him, as J confessed, in the last semester of his Senior year of high school, the head librarian caught him in the midst of his "editing" and thereafter banned him from the library. J insisted that he was doing nothing wrong, rather quite the opposite, making critical corrections, but the librarian would not be dissuaded from her position and, after adjusting her wire-frame glasses on the narrow bridge of her nose, she demanded J give her his library card, which he did, and then she tore it to shreds in front of him and insisted in a shrill voice that he leave immediately or she would call the Principal's office.

No doubt it's significant that J's conviction that he could edit text mentally, beyond scribbling his edits in library books by hand, only began to manifest itself just after his father died.

Perhaps in this way death was no deterrent for J in trying to fix the problem of relating to his father. Indeed, it seemed his father's death intensified J's longing to the point where his childhood eigth-grade recollection of editing changes having kept his father home from work and closer to him had somehow, no doubt at some subconscious level, advanced in J's mind to the point of his harboring the notion that he could alter printed text physically via his mind or psyche, in order to sidestep the very real and otherwise unavoidable reality of his father's death.

By giving the skill of mental revision a physical dimension, J was symbolically nullifying the physical reality of his father's death. He simply wanted his father to be alive again and for himself to realize the potential he never fully achieved in his lifetime of being close to his father—a potential so many sons harbor, frequently strive toward and fail at, then must accept never fully having realized. But J was having trouble with the latter portion of this sadly all-too-common father/son dynamic—accepting failure at never having achieved a true and meaningful bond with his father.

11.
Poster from One of Abram's Magic Shows

July 7, 1981

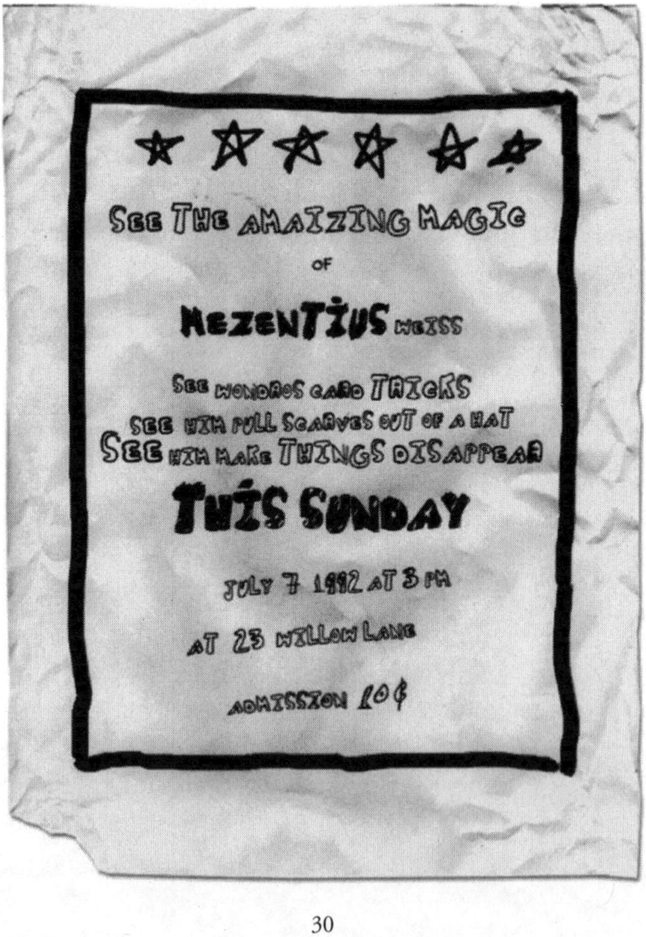

12.
The Diary of Dr. Isaac Himmelfarb

June 9, 2018

Looking back at my last diary entry, I wonder now: what did I know at eight when I first got to know Abram and Sara? I thought Abram's fascination with magic and his idea of changing Superman stories were cool and little Sara captivated me from the first moment we met. Since I was an only child and my father had committed suicide when I was ten years old, the entire Weiss family intrigued me because they seemed truly intact, not broken like my family, which consisted of just my mom and me. I was especially curious about their father, Zach, although when I was a boy he seemed a bit distant, detached from all save his work, with which he was clearly obsessed. Although I can now recall Zach, after my dad killed himself, sometimes seeming to study me when I was a boy playing with his children in his home. No doubt, with 20/20 hindsight, given the nature of my father's death, it was with professional curiosity that Zach looked upon me. Considering it today, I wonder if Zach was aware of his son Abram's notion of changing storylines in his Superman comic books, which might have opened the door a crack to his later professional encounter with his patient J?

Their older brother, Joshua, wanted to be like his dad, a doctor, a psychiatrist, who I rarely interacted with, but Abram and Sara, twins, were the same age as me, and so we three were often together, especially when Abram put on his magic shows. The first time Abram put on a magic show for the public in his backyard, Abram's father, Zach, disapproved. I vividly remember at the time overhearing Zach vehemently telling Joshua that Abram's interest in magic was illogical nonsense and he ought to go tell his younger brother to abandon such stupidity. Joshua gamely tried to dissuade Abram from putting on his magic show, but there was nothing anyone could say to persuade Abram that magic wasn't real and reality couldn't be altered. So the show went on, as did several others, despite Zach's adamant disapproval, which struck me then, even as a young boy, as way out of proportion to something so innocent and playful as a kid's magic show. Even then, I wondered if the entire concept of magic somehow challenged Zach's view of the universe in a way that fed off of his obsession with his work as a psychiatrist.

Looking back on it now, I see that Sara held the three of us—herself, her brother Abram, and me—together. Indeed, Sara's earliest overtures were geared towards helping me and helping Abram. But, how can I help her now?

13.
Transcript of Message Left on Dr. Himmelfarb's Answering Machine

June 11, 2018

Phone Message:
Dr. Himmelfarb, this is your mother-in-law's nurse, Glenda Kravitz. I don't want to disturb you, but I thought you should know, I was with your mother-in-law late last night and was surprised to see your wife, Sara, drop by unannounced. No one told me to expect her, so I wanted to get back to you about what happened. As you know, given your mother-in-law's advancing Alzheimer's, she's prone to sudden rages, especially if surprised by anything or anyone. I'm sorry to say that your wife's dropping by upset your mother-in-law, Mrs. Weiss, a lot. I don't know what else to tell you, other than to put it plainly: your mother-in-law was very agitated by your wife's appearance in the house. Sadly, Mrs. Weiss did not recognize her own daughter, your wife, called her a "damned hussy," then asked Sara, "How the hell do you know my husband, Zach? Do you take me for a fool? I've known your kind before and seen them coming from a mile away. My husband doesn't truly care for you. How dare you enter our home?"

It was horribly sad and awkward to remind your mother-in-law that her husband, Zach, was not there, while dodging the fact that her husband was recently deceased, and trying to explain to Mrs. Weiss that the visitor was her daughter. I hate to leave this message on your machine, but wanted to let you know for the future, if either of you are going to drop by, it might be best if you let me know in advance and perhaps it might be best if you accompany Sara when she wants to visit her mother. Well, that's it, bye.

14.
Esther Weiss's Day Planner,

April 11, 1990

<u>Sunday, April 11</u>

Zach

1. Does he have enough typing paper for office?
2. Check suits sent to cleaners. Check socks, shirts and underwear for the week.
3. Zach's as bad as the kids—dirty clothes go in bathroom hamper.

Myself

1. Get extra lamb roast for Thursday dinner with Nicolsons.
2. Leave 50 dollars for Maria.
3. Spot check boys' rooms again. Make sure beds made.
4. Check Sara's closet, better than boys about neatness.
5. Make sure children are doing lessons.

Joshua

1. See if he can mow lawn and take out garbage.
2. See if he has time to help Abram with Hebrew for hour.
3. Get him to talk about this Judith Syms girl who's stuck mash notes in school books. Fifteen is too early to be serious about girls.

Abram

1. See he's prepped for Hebrew School and done other schoolwork.
2. Keep weaning him from comic books. Give him 100 Best-Loved Poems .
3. See if comic books can be tossed today without him noticing. I did wean him from bottle like that when he was baby.
4. Look for books in Zach's library encouraging logical thought. Plato maybe? See what his friend, Isaac reads, must be ok.

Sara

1. See that she works on assignments 7 P.M. to 9 P.M. bedtime. Get her into good regular study habits. Seems slower than Josh and Abram.

15.
Notes from *The Revisionist: A Case of Logokinesis Mania*

Dr. Zachary Weiss

As our sessions progressed together, it became more and more clear that the stressor, or proverbial straw that broke the camel's back, for J was the death of his father. J's formative years of enduring frustration in trying to gain his father's respect and attention, combined with his alienation from his mother, had significantly contributed to the development of his actually believing he had the mental or psychic capacity to alter words on the page.

Having never encountered a patient with this specific delusion, I looked through various medical dictionaries trying to find a term that might fit J's condition. In the end, in the absence of any previously defined name that coincided specifically with the singularly peculiar aspect of J's condition, I came to the conclusion that I would have to figure out a precise phrase or term of my own that was accurately representative of the symptoms J was both suffering from and enduring. I realized that whatever name for his condition I came up with, it would have to combine the obsession with words with something describing the process of actually physically altering printed text, or at least believing one was altering the text. The Greek root, logo-, meaning word, would have to be part of that word. Then, it came to me; the word had to be Logokinesis. It would be a neologism combining the Greek for word with the Greek term for motion, movement. I would then define it as the belief that one had the ability to alter the printed word physically. Such an obsession with a delusional belief could be classified as a mania. Thus, J's condition I would term, Logokenesis Mania.

Unlike the plethora of housewives hitting my office couch with their complaints about cheating husbands and the frailty or absolute death of "real love," or my garden-variety patient run of drug-addled adolescents from wealthy families wrestling aimlessly with their identities, J's case was in another realm altogether.

J's Logokinesis Mania was the sort of case one in my field might, if he were fortunate, encounter once in a career. As a starting point, I launched my analysis from the point of view that J's yearning to be noticed by his father while he was still alive was intensified by his father's frequent absences due to his job. When J's father died, he was lost to J forever—however, J's yearning was not lost, or even diminished, but rather intensified. Thus leaving J to contrive his Logokinesis Mania as an ongoing connection to his deceased father. My job, if I was to figure how the hell to handle it, was to help J let go of his Logokinesis Mania and accept the death of his father, but J was deeply entrenched in his delusional thinking and fought me at every turn whenever I suggested the slightest possibility that his supposed psychic ability to alter words on a page might be, to say the least, a dubious capacity.

As our sessions progressed over the next year, it became readily apparent that J blamed his mother for driving his father away with her incessant nagging that his father be more ambitious and make more money. Finally, J's parents divorced when J was 16, in the midst of high school and, after that, as mentioned above, J launched his adolescent handwritten editorial career with library books, quite likely driven at some unconscious level by the recollection of how it was editorial errors in a book his father was selling that had kept his father home, closer to J, offering, at the least, by his proximity, the potential of father and son growing closer. So was that it? In the back of his head, did J harbor the notion that editorial changes could somehow facilitate a closing of the gulf he felt between himself and his detached father?

Afterward, when J went off to college, he spent as much time as possible during his college years visiting his father on holidays, as well as spring and summer breaks. His father, J told me, staring at the carpet in my office, never remarried and swore to his dying day that J's mother was the love of his life. On the other hand, J rarely visited his mother, who was more interested in starting a new life in Boston than keeping in touch with family. When his mother remarried a very wealthy investment banker who had also recently divorced and ended up with custody of his son from his previous marriage (who, by odd coincidence, was exactly the same age as J), J cut off what little contact he had with his mother, whom he witnessed doting on her new husband's son while ignoring J.

As we spoke of his mother, it was quickly apparent that J harbored intense hatred towards her. I fathom, beyond J's resentment of his mother's apparent abandonment of him for her new stepson, there was also a very real and concrete defense with which J was wrestling, against a mutually unconscious incestuous desire on the part of both mother and son. J said that his mother had kept her figure trim through diet and exercise and knew how to catch men's attention when she put her hand on her waist, tilted her hips to one side then took a breath, drew her shoulders back, showcasing her ample breasts, while offering a pouting smile and a charming tilt of her head. J confessed he found it deeply upsetting that he had to admit his mom had real sex appeal.

"I hope you don't think my telling you this means I had any actual, weird physical desires for my mother. I know I may not be the most normal guy on the planet, but that sort of thing never truly entered my mind!" J stared across my desk as he emphatically uttered these words.

An interesting side note: J, in other sessions, admitted he had dated two older women, whom he described as very sexy and both obsessed with literature, although each left him in the end for wealthier, older men.

When I finally pressed J to reveal when he first came to have the conviction that he could alter language on the page through his mind or psyche, he confessed it was after his father's funeral. At that point, J was twenty-seven and already an editor at Banner Books. At the funeral, he'd seen his mother for the last time. She and her new husband arrived dressed in clothes that put all of J's father's friends and family to shame.

Where most of the men had to make do with their J.C. Penny suits and the women with ill-fitting discount dresses that hardly flattered their figures, J's mother was wearing a tightly fitted, perfectly tailored Chanel black dress. Her new husband had on a dark pinstripe Armani suit.

J recalled that he left the funeral in a rage. What he found helped assuage his anger when he returned to his apartment was re-reading his favorite book, Kafka's *Metamorphosis*, editing the opening lines again and again in his mind, then seeing the words on the page change.

At this point, I understood how my earliest responses to J fell in with conventional medical practice. This entailed my initial course of treatment of medicating J with Rispidal and Xanax to suppress his revisionist delusions and the anxieties they provoked, along with Zoloft to combat his depression. But as our sessions progressed, I became more and more preoccupied, outside of our sessions, with thoughts of J and his insistence that he actually could achieve Logokinesis Mania, and for the first time in my career, I seriously wrestled with doubts as to the prudence of the course of treatment I was providing to this patient.

16.
The Diary of Isaac Himmelfarb

June 4, 2018

Slogging through the boxes of Zach's papers, I'm starting to get a glimpse of what triggered Zach's obsession with his patient J. The disappearance or malleability of what we accept as a given—something true, as if permanently printed on the pages of our lives—isn't that precisely what Zach's patient J challenged him with at the end of his career? Yet oddly, it now strikes me, all those years before J showed up in Zach's office, wasn't this exactly the same issue that Zach's own son, Abram, was wrestling with in Zach's own backyard?

When we were kids, Sara was Abram's assistant in his magic shows in their backyard. Abram was good at pulling scarves out of an empty hat or his sleeve. But a real magician, he said, would be able to cast a spell like, "Abracadabra, let my parents like magic," and so it'd be. He wanted real powers, to be able somehow to access the malleability of what everyone else around him accepted as "real." In the end, Abram was fascinated by what he deemed the ultimate classic trick during a magic show: Making someone or something disappear or change!

Oddly, looking back over the years today, without a father or any siblings of my own, my next-door neighbors, the Weiss family, with whom I was so fascinated, performed their own sort of vanishing show over the years. First, Sara's eldest brother, Joshua, vanished when he died in that car crash in college, and Abram later followed suit, not dying so far as we knew, but dropping out of college and disappearing. Sara was then alone, beyond me, later her husband, with just her mother and father, the one fading to Alzheimer's, the other to cancer. The only hope for the future—for an appearance rather than another disappearance—had been in Sara's womb.

But now, with the not unexpected death of her father, my dear Sara is left still facing the ultimate blow, in the depths of her massive depression from her miscarriage, trying to live with the loss of our baby she was carrying.

17.
Liquor Receipt for Sara Himmelfarb

6/10/18

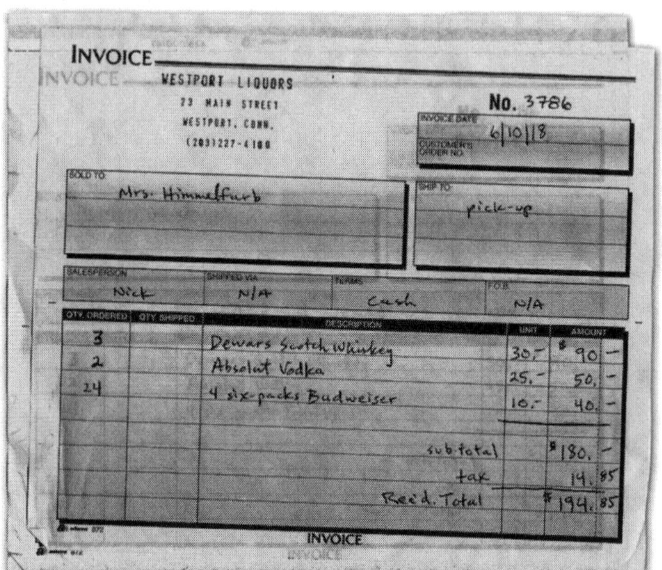

INVOICE

WESTPORT LIQUORS
73 MAIN STREET
WESTPORT, CONN.
(203)227-4188

No. 3786

INVOICE DATE: 6/10/18
CUSTOMER'S ORDER NO.:

SOLD TO: Mrs. Himmelfarb

SHIP TO: pick-up

SALESPERSON	SHIPPED VIA	TERMS	F.O.B.
Nick	N/A	Cash	N/A

QTY. ORDERED	QTY. SHIPPED	DESCRIPTION	UNIT	AMOUNT
3		Dewars Scotch Whiskey	30.-	$90.-
2		Absolut Vodka	25.-	50.-
24		4 six-packs Budweiser	10.-	40.-
		sub total		$180.-
		tax		14.85
		Rec'd. Total		$194.85

INVOICE

18.
Death Certificate for Isaac Himmelfarb's Father

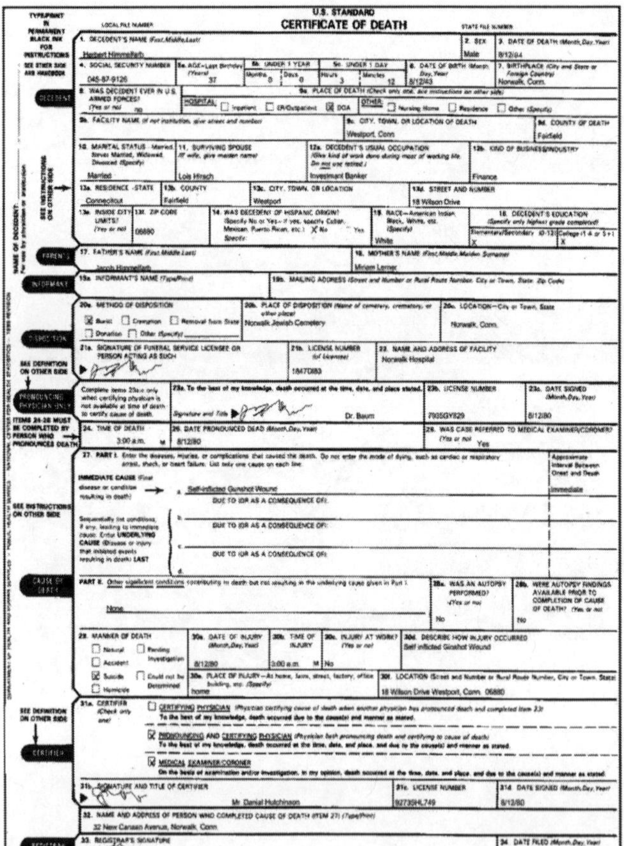

U.S. STANDARD
CERTIFICATE OF DEATH

LOCAL FILE NUMBER
STATE FILE NUMBER

- 1. DECEDENT'S NAME (First, Middle, Last): Herbert Himmelfarb
- 2. SEX: Male
- 3. DATE OF DEATH (Month, Day, Year): 8/12/84
- 4. SOCIAL SECURITY NUMBER: 045-87-9126
- 5a. AGE—Last Birthday (Years): 37
- 5b. UNDER 1 YEAR: Months 0, Days 0
- 5c. UNDER 1 DAY: Hours 3, Minutes 12
- 6. DATE OF BIRTH (Month, Day, Year): 8/12/43
- 7. BIRTHPLACE (City and State or Foreign Country): Norwalk, Conn.
- 8. WAS DECEDENT EVER IN U.S. ARMED FORCES? (Yes or no): no
- 9a. PLACE OF DEATH (Check only one): HOSPITAL: Inpatient / ER/Outpatient / [X] DOA; OTHER: Nursing Home / Residence / Other (Specify)
- 9b. FACILITY NAME (If not institution, give street and number)
- 9c. CITY, TOWN, OR LOCATION OF DEATH: Westport, Conn
- 9d. COUNTY OF DEATH: Fairfield
- 10. MARITAL STATUS—Married, Never Married, Widowed, Divorced (Specify): Married
- 11. SURVIVING SPOUSE (If wife, give maiden name): Lois Hirsch
- 12a. DECEDENT'S USUAL OCCUPATION (Give kind of work done during most of working life. Do not use retired.): Investment Banker
- 12b. KIND OF BUSINESS/INDUSTRY: Finance
- 13a. RESIDENCE—STATE: Connecticut
- 13b. COUNTY: Fairfield
- 13c. CITY, TOWN, OR LOCATION: Westport
- 13d. STREET AND NUMBER: 18 Wilson Drive
- 13e. INSIDE CITY LIMITS? (Yes or no)
- 13f. ZIP CODE: 06880
- 14. WAS DECEDENT OF HISPANIC ORIGIN? (Specify No or Yes—If yes, specify Cuban, Mexican, Puerto Rican, etc.): [X] No / Yes; Specify:
- 15. RACE—American Indian, Black, White, etc. (Specify): White
- 16. DECEDENT'S EDUCATION (Specify only highest grade completed): Elementary/Secondary (0-12): X; College (1-4 or 5+): X
- 17. FATHER'S NAME (First, Middle, Last): Jacob Himmelfarb
- 18. MOTHER'S NAME (First, Middle, Maiden Surname): Miriam Lerner
- 19a. INFORMANT'S NAME (Type/Print)
- 19b. MAILING ADDRESS (Street and Number or Rural Route Number, City or Town, State, Zip Code)
- 20a. METHOD OF DISPOSITION: [X] Burial / Cremation / Removal from State / Donation / Other (Specify)
- 20b. PLACE OF DISPOSITION (Name of cemetery, crematory, or other place): Norwalk Jewish Cemetery
- 20c. LOCATION—City or Town, State: Norwalk, Conn.
- 21a. SIGNATURE OF FUNERAL SERVICE LICENSEE OR PERSON ACTING AS SUCH: [signature]
- 21b. LICENSE NUMBER (of Licensee): 1847D83
- 22. NAME AND ADDRESS OF FACILITY: Norwalk Hospital

Complete items 23a-c only when certifying physician is not available at time of death to certify cause of death.

- 23a. To the best of my knowledge, death occurred at the time, date, and place stated. Signature and Title: [signature] Dr. Baum
- 23b. LICENSE NUMBER: 7935GY829
- 23c. DATE SIGNED (Month, Day, Year): 8/12/80

ITEMS 24-26 MUST BE COMPLETED BY PERSON WHO PRONOUNCES DEATH

- 24. TIME OF DEATH: 3:00 a.m. M
- 25. DATE PRONOUNCED DEAD (Month, Day, Year): 8/12/80
- 26. WAS CASE REFERRED TO MEDICAL EXAMINER/CORONER? (Yes or no): Yes
- 27. PART I. Enter the diseases, injuries, or complications that caused the death. Do not enter the mode of dying, such as cardiac or respiratory arrest, shock, or heart failure. List only one cause on each line.
  - IMMEDIATE CAUSE (Final disease or condition resulting in death) → a. Self-inflicted Gunshot Wound — Approximate Interval Between Onset and Death: Immediate
  - DUE TO (OR AS A CONSEQUENCE OF):
  - Sequentially list conditions, if any, leading to immediate cause. Enter UNDERLYING CAUSE (Disease or injury that initiated events resulting in death) LAST — b. DUE TO (OR AS A CONSEQUENCE OF): c. DUE TO (OR AS A CONSEQUENCE OF): d.
- PART II. Other significant conditions contributing to death but not resulting in the underlying cause given in Part I.: None
- 28a. WAS AN AUTOPSY PERFORMED? (Yes or no): No
- 28b. WERE AUTOPSY FINDINGS AVAILABLE PRIOR TO COMPLETION OF CAUSE OF DEATH? (Yes or no): No
- 29. MANNER OF DEATH: Natural / Pending Investigation / Accident / [X] Suicide / Could not be Determined / Homicide
- 30a. DATE OF INJURY (Month, Day, Year): 8/12/80
- 30b. TIME OF INJURY: 3:00 a.m. M
- 30c. INJURY AT WORK? (Yes or no): No
- 30d. DESCRIBE HOW INJURY OCCURRED: Self inflicted Ginshot Wound
- 30e. PLACE OF INJURY—At home, farm, street, factory, office building, etc. (Specify): home
- 30f. LOCATION (Street and Number or Rural Route Number, City or Town, State): 18 Wilson Drive Westport, Conn. 06880
- 31a. CERTIFIER (Check only one)
  - [ ] CERTIFYING PHYSICIAN (Physician certifying cause of death when another physician has pronounced death and completed Item 23) To the best of my knowledge, death occurred due to the cause(s) and manner as stated.
  - [X] PRONOUNCING AND CERTIFYING PHYSICIAN (Physician both pronouncing death and certifying to cause of death) To the best of my knowledge, death occurred at the time, date, and place, and due to the cause(s) and manner as stated.
  - [X] MEDICAL EXAMINER/CORONER On the basis of examination and/or investigation, in my opinion, death occurred at the time, date, and place, and due to the cause(s) and manner as stated.
- 31b. SIGNATURE AND TITLE OF CERTIFIER: [signature] Mr. Danial Hutchinson
- 31c. LICENSE NUMBER: 92735HL749
- 31d. DATE SIGNED (Month, Day, Year): 8/12/80
- 32. NAME AND ADDRESS OF PERSON WHO COMPLETED CAUSE OF DEATH (ITEM 27) (Type/Print): 32 New Canaan Avenue, Norwalk, Conn
- 33. REGISTRAR'S SIGNATURE: [signature]
- 34. DATE FILED (Month, Day, Year): 8/12/80

PHS-T 003

19.
Letter from Isaac Himmelfarb to Sara Weiss

August 14, 1994

Dear Sara,

I can't express how grateful I was that G-d put you here on this planet, next door to me. My father's funeral, yesterday, was the saddest day for me. Yet, even though I told you, you didn't have to come, you came anyway with your mom and dad and Abram. I'm writing to you to say how glad I am you didn't listen to me. If you hadn't been there, I would've felt so alone.

No one mentioned it, either there or later, but you know me, and I wonder if you guessed that my father's death was something I blamed myself for. His death, I overheard the grown-ups say, was due to suicide. But I also heard another word mentioned: drink. His doctor, they said, had warned him, he was developing trouble with his liver, but my dad never paid much attention to doctors and mostly, I felt, was disappointed by me. Now, I'm left wondering: Did I disappoint him that much?

When the grown-ups were talking, the Rabbi was there and they were talking about how if you take your own life you're not supposed to be buried in a Jewish cemetery, but then the Rabbi said the new view is if someone kills themselves they weren't of sound mind so a normal Jewish burial could be done. Truth is—I don't know that my dad would've given a damn how he was buried, but I saw how the whole talk upset my mom and felt bad for her.

Seeing how sad my mom was, I just felt numb, like after you bump your knee into something and your knee just tingles—except here my whole body felt weird. I was also sad in the cemetery that so few people showed up for my dad's burial. I realized we just barely made a Minyan to say Kaddish over his grave. Most of the people you saw there were some of his old business associates. Hardly any of his family members made it to the cemetery. Even Dad's brother, my Uncle Manny, my dad's only brother, didn't make it. When he called the next week and I spoke to him on the phone, he said he was sorry, but he'd been buried with too much work at the office.

You remember the Rabbi? You nailed it actually when you said he seemed like he didn't know who my dad was, but I was too numb to answer you at my dad's grave. As you know, he wasn't our Rabbi Rubenstien, who was laid up with pneumonia, but a substitute/stand-in Rabbi, who never met or said two words to my dad. So, my dad was buried by a stranger.

Anyone who isn't totally nuts should express some sorrow, some sense of loss when they lose their dad. Honor your mother and father, Moses was told by G-d on Mount Sinai—I know that's what they tell us in Hebrew school, but I'm confused: did I honor my father enough or not? Just exactly what am I supposed to feel right now?

I'm so lucky to have you as a part of my life, even if this note sounds a bit nuts. I've no idea who I could turn to and share these weird feelings with, if not you.

Thanks for being there for me,
Isaac

20.
Notes from *The Revisionist: A Case of Logokinesis Mania*

Dr. Zachary Weiss

I had been treating J for what I deemed was his psychosis for about five months when J confessed he was unhappy with the course of his therapy. When I asked him why, he said he felt the drugs made him emotionally numb and unable to concentrate on his work. J even intimated that he might lose his job if things didn't improve. He then requested that I reduce the dosage of his medications so that he wouldn't feel so flat and wouldn't jeopardize his job.

I didn't wish to argue, but had to point out to J that he'd displayed no interest in his delusional revisionist fantasy for months since his medications had taken full effect. Nor had he shown any of the manic tendencies associated with his delusion. I suggested it would not be prudent for me as a physician to alter what seemed to be working.

However, J reiterated that the medications were interfering with his editing work and taking all pleasure out of his life. When I still resisted, J said he could show me how much his work had deteriorated under his current medication regime. He offered to show me a copy of a manuscript he had edited before his medications took full effect and another manuscript he'd worked on since the medications took effect.

I thought this was only fair and agreed that I would look over the manuscripts before our next session and that we could revisit our discussion of his medications at that time. He had already brought in the two manuscripts with his handwritten notes on them. So, after he agreed to my proposal, he handed me the manuscripts.

After J left my office, as he was my last appointment that day, I immediately began poring over the work J had left with me, like a detective, searching his syllables for any clues I might discern that would offer me more insight into my most unique patient. The works in question were fiction pieces. J had written on the title page of each manuscript the dates on which he worked on each piece and some of his responses. I was sorry to see, after a cursory examination of the manuscripts, that J was right: his editing work showed an alarming decline in quality, to say the least. Where the earliest manuscript bristled with good to excellent suggestions for tightening narrative flow and improving characterizations, the later manuscript revealed haphazard and even confused edits which indicated J was not clear what the story he had been reading was about.

Sadly, no matter how long I read and re-read his editorial notes and paced my office pondering them while searching for a connection to J's conviction that he could alter printed text with his mind, I came away no closer to understanding J's Logokinesis Mania, which, since our first session, he'd been dodging speaking of directly almost entirely.

In our next session, on the basis of my review of J's two manuscripts, I proposed to J that we gradually reduce the medications over the next month by about a third and see how well he responded to that. J thought that reasonable and agreed.

Indeed, towards the end of that month I noticed that J's attitude and manner was definitely improving. His mode of conversation became more animated. He began cracking jokes and engaging in company gossip, which he'd never done before. He told me that his office was pleased with his improved productivity. He claimed that he found he could again analyze submitted work more closely and could make helpful editing comments to the authors whose work he was reviewing.

I was pleased and thought I had succeeded in rekindling J's love and talent for his work by a judicious reduction in his medications, until half-way through the second month of what I thought was my new and appropriate medical regime for J, when J brought up his revisionist fantasy again, disabusing me of my sense of triumph.

This time J said that at work he'd thought to see pages of text reflecting what he was thinking they should reflect. But then, a moment later, upon closer scrutiny, he realized the text had not changed. What he saw was what he *imagined* the text should read.

I was not deceived. After careful questioning, it was clear that J once again believed in his delusion. When I suggested that reducing the dosage of his medications might be the cause of his Logokinetic illusions, J said he would NOT change the medication dosage and go back to that dead, unfeeling state of mind he had suffered from before. On this, he was adamant and, to my shock, for the first time in the course of treating him, when I returned to the question of his medication, J suddenly stood up and left my office half-way through our session, slamming the door behind him.

21.
Novel Edited by J Before Medications Took Effect (Title Page)

Word count: 15,650
Herbert Selden Tusker
14 Maple Lane,
Barnston, Nebraska
35689

Benvenuto's Welcome. A Novel of the Renaissance
By Herbert Tusker

— Good grasp of seventeenth-century Florentine Politics
— Story marred by giving Cellini a fictional sidekick,
— Worse, name of sidekick—Pazzo—crazy.
— Fictive sidekick acts too flippant, too modern
— With Cellini—Real Cellini would have killed this guy.
— Change name of sidekick to something neutral like Roberto and make clear his social class in relation to Cellini.
— Not clear if he's a servant, apprentice or what?
— Would have mattered to Cellini
— Cut down on internal reflection by sidekick Pazzo, doesn't move story forward.
— Suggestion for revision: Have each chapter correspond to a city visited by Cellini. Rome, Paris, etc.

— Cut down on historical sidebars and integrate better to narrative, examples shown in text.
— Too much technical jargon about sculpting and metal working, liable to lose reader, use simpler and more precise descriptions of Cellini's technical skills, examples highlighted in text.
— Watch out for verbal anachronisms. Cellini would never say, "That's truly wild," in conversation. He's not a character on *Friends*. Again, examples highlighted.
— Too many adverbs! See individual line edits.

22.
Novel Edited by J After Medications Took Effect (Title Page)

Word count:18,789
Stanley Zolinsky
240 East 86th Street
Apt. 14J
New York, New York
10028

The Zebra Wore Stripes
By Stanley Zolinsky

— some sort of murder mystery
— Zebra not mentioned
— IF you mention the Zebra, then WHAT IS HIS MOTIVATION?
—Zoo setting
— story starts at night
— body found in daylight
— Don't remember when murder happened
— just a body, name is Joe, maybe James
— He has stripes, what would he wear? Plaid?

Hey Pierce, What the hell is this? Are you drinking? We have to talk—Pronto!
Ed.

23.
The Diary of Isaac Himmelfarb

June 12, 2018

DAMN! DAMN! DAMN! 'Where the HELL is she?' I keep asking myself—knowing I can't take much more of this. It's been a week since Sara's been out all hours without explaining her late, drunken returns home. Just staggering past me when she returns, then collapsing on our bed and often passing out fully dressed. And what have I done about it? Nothing, nada, zip—well, no more! Tonight I decided, I can't be my wife's enabler, just watching her let her life go to hell, so I headed over to her childhood home at three in the morning to look for her there.

Sure enough, I found Sara, drunk out of her mind, in her old room, where she was splayed out on her childhood bed, limbs at odd angles, squinting at me through bloodshot eyes. I then noticed on the floor of her closet, which was open, a collection of empty Vodka bottles. Getting her back to our house was no easy task, but I somehow managed it and, once we were back in our own house, in our own bedroom, I tried to get her to sleep. But Sara resisted the notion of sleeping and, in her stupor, she started coming on to me, leaning up against me, brushing her breasts against my chest while reaching for my crotch.

Despite Sara's liquor breath, I have to admit it turned me on, and so we sort of undressed—my pants half-off, her panties gone and skirt pulled up, shirt unbuttoned—then we fell down on the bed and started going at it. I felt the heat of her body flushed, her full, round breasts; it was exciting, and as I started touching her, feeling her, she was moaning. After I'd already entered her and was starting to increase my rhythm, she shouted, "Uh! Uh!"—I thought she liked it, I liked it—

Then she screamed, "Get the fuck off me," grabbed my shoulders and pushed me up, like she was doing some aerobic pushup. As she threw herself out of the bed, I tumbled from the bed and slid to the floor dragging sheets, bed covers and clothes with me. There I lay, tangled in linen as I listened to Sara vomiting into the toilet.

Eventually, Sara staggered out of the bathroom. When I disentangled myself and stood up, I offered her my hand as she leaned, swaying slightly, against the bathroom's doorframe, but she slapped my hand away, slurring out, "Aw, fuck it, Ize," somehow wobbled a step toward our bed, then fell over onto it and passed out.

I can see the sun just starting to rise through our bedroom curtains at this point, but I can't sleep. I've been sitting here wondering if Sara has now cast me as a sort of father substitute since Zach's death—and just how odd might that be when considering, with hindsight, after my own father's suicide I had looked to Zach for a father substitute?

Yet, I suspect seeking a father substitute after the death of one's father is not terribly aberrant, however what Zach might have found to be quite unique in J's case is precisely that J did not seek a father substitute after his father's death, but instead looked for and believed he had found a bridge to his dead father, via his Logokinesis Mania. Thus, looking at Zach's J, it's clear that, absent an actual living man on whom he might choose to project a classic father substitute construct, he chose instead to pursue a psychological *bridge* to his dead father via his revisionist fantasies. Sadly, all of J's revisionist fantasies failed to supply J with the love he lacked from his dead father since the fantasies were an evasion rather than a confrontation with the reality of his father's death.

I'd also my own early brush with death when I lost my father, just as Sara has had her brushes with death in the loss of her brother, Josh, then our baby she was carrying, and then her father, Zach. But where Sara and I faced death with its overwhelming weight of *disappointment*, J's response to the death of his father seems to have resulted in *actual psychosis*. In reviewing Zach's papers, it's definitely becoming clear that death figured significantly in the development of the psychotic aspects of J's revisionist fantasies.

Since J's father's death brought home to J the love he would never experience, he compensated in an effort to avoid that reality by intensifying his editing fantasies to the perceptual level of what he perceived as "reality." To revive an opportunity to connect with his deceased father, albeit a sort of psychological sidestepping of the actual reality of his father's death, J must have had no doubts about his ability to alter printed text mentally; he needed truly to believe he had Logokinetic powers which, as I've been reading Zach's notes, it seems Zach himself also came to entertain in the end.

24.
Letter from Sara to Her Parents, Zach and Esther Weiss

November 13, 2002

Dear Mom and Dad,

As I told you last week, I've been trying to reach Abram, but have been having trouble getting him on the phone. The one time I got Abram he did that silly trick of pretending there was too much static on the line for us to talk. When I told him to quit it, he just said he couldn't hear me and had to hang up. So I decided to go up to Cambridge and try speak with him in person.

When I arrived, he was not in his dorm room or the library, so I wandered about campus looking for him. Finally, I saw him in Harvard Square yesterday. He was across the street, staring at the sidewalk while walking rapidly, as if oblivious to his surroundings. He was also dressed very oddly: he had on an ill-fitting brown tweed jacket, a stained and wrinkled white shirt with a small red bow tie, torn chinos and sandals. His beard is now long and scraggly, like his hair, which is all over the place. I called out to him but he didn't respond and, when I tried to approach him, just as I was crossing the street, he ran off.

He looks strange and I think he needs help. Daddy, I know you'll come up with a good plan. You've got to. I've enclosed a drawing I tried to make of Abram the way he looked yesterday. He looks so lost

Lots of love,
Sara

25.
Abram's Letter to His Father, Zach

Undated, c. 2002

Undear false one,

Even after losing my brother, Josh, you wouldn't listen to me—ripped up my heart and my soul sending me to this GODDLESS place, this Place worshipped as Harvard—the rotted fruit corrupting the souls of those who may still be angelic on the faithless globe, the bag of fucking filth—This eye, this I, I was meant for so much more than the maunderings of gibbering fleshy husks, soulless Golems claiming to be professors but PROFESSING nothing but dreck wrapt round their wormy egos—You left me bereft of a place to go, but compelled by an overwhelming need, an irresistible itch to scratch till bleeding and go—anywhere the hell that isn't here—

You know You know but say NOTHING, nothing. You send spies to Cambridge disguised as Sara, but I'm on to your game! Stop it! I was meant for more—You ABRAHAM MOLOCH—when you wielded the blade, you thought it was memememememe the ISAAC tho dubbed ABRAM but it was POOR JOSHUA the brother damned—It was me you wanted to be dead but you struck at a chosen one and another died—Father, Please Fix me, Please Fix me, Please Fix

memememememememememememememememememememememe o please, fix me———

ABRAM—ABRAHAM—ABRA—ABRA—cadave—the past is erased—fill in the blanks!!!

ABRA CADAVER ABRAM

26.
The Diary of Isaac Himmelfarb

June 15, 2018

Going through the massive collection of documents Zach kept in these cardboard boxes presents me with the ultimate (and often painful) trip down Memory Lane. Having just read Sara's old letter to her parents and then staring and staring at Abram's last incoherent letter to his father before he disappeared, it strikes me now that I must make some effort to track down Abram to let him know his father has passed away. But where and how the hell do I begin to track Abram down?

I know that by December of 2002, Abram had left Cambridge, dropped out of Harvard, dropped off the map, but after that everything was sketchy. No one had any idea where he'd gone. I recall how, at the time, both Sara and I wondered if Zach had hired some private detectives to look for Abram, but Zach never wanted to talk about Abram. In fact, if anyone hazarded any comment or question about Abram over the dinner table back then, Zach would only offer an audible groan or muttered curse, push back his chair, rise, and leave the table, often with his plate of food only half-touched.

My own mom tried to console me that year, recalling our common struggle to accept the disappearance of my father from our lives. But my father's disappearance was definite and would never change, while Abram's disappearance remained an unsolved mystery. At one point my mother remarked, after Abram's initial disappearance, "He was such a sweet and shy boy, but, you know, he was always a little peculiar. Maybe Zach found a nice facility to take care of him?"

My dear Sara's brother's disappearance did bring back recollections to me of my feelings after my dad was gone of being unable to do anything, being entirely ineffectual, at a loss as to how to help, but for the sake of Sara, I kept these thoughts to myself and tried to be as emotionally supportive as I could be in her time of need—her time of struggling to accept the utter uncertainty as to where her brother, Abram, might be.

27.
Notes from *The Revisionist: A Case of Logokinesis Mania*

Dr. Zachary Weiss

After J's abrupt and angry departure from our session where we last spoke of returning his meds to a higher dosage, which he insisted he would not do, I acceded to J's wishes and observed him closely over the next two months after reducing his meds by a third. Finally, J offered to show me samples of his recent work to demonstrate that the renewed success he was having in editing was genuine.

Before our next session, I reviewed the recent work he'd left with me. Immediately after taking his seat in my office at our next session, he asked what I thought of his recent work. I admitted to J, "Your editing work on the collection of short stories you left with me is brilliant. Of course, I am not a professional editor, but I am an avid reader and, as such, I can think of no other word for your editing. You trimmed unnecessary details out of the stories, made excellent notes on how to make the characters more consistent and had great suggestions for better physical descriptions of the characters. You even clarified and made cleaner and smoother the dramatic arc within each story."

J smiled at me and softly said, "I was right about the meds after all, wasn't I?"

I reluctantly nodded and admitted that I was "cautiously optimistic for the present with his current course of treatment."

Then, without missing a beat, he asked, "Isn't it time I showed you how good an editor I really can be?"

Suddenly I felt an onset of anxiety as I feared he would now offer to show me how he could edit printed texts by will power alone.

As if having read my thoughts, J hesitated then replied in a lower voice, "You know and I know that all this time you've just been waiting to see me alter printed text by my will power alone. Go ahead, tell me that's not true?"

"I thought I had made it clear from the beginning that I cannot permit you to attempt to do that precisely because it would only encourage this belief of yours. In fact, I felt it was a sign of progress that you had stopped speaking of this belief as our work here together progressed."

J just scowled and waved his right hand, "Oh, come on doctor, I'm a big boy. Just pick out a book, any book you have here, select a page for me to read and I'll change passages on that page for you and show you I'm not delusional."

"It's true, your morale and editing abilities at your job have clearly improved. But what if I agree to your demand and you are unable to succeed in anything more than demonstrating conclusively the illusionary state of your belief? I worry that I would be irresponsible if I permit the highly foreseeable likelihood of that happening. Please suppose, as I believe, you wouldn't be able to do it: how well would you handle it? At a stroke, in one session, we could undo all the good work we've accomplished so far."

At that, J grew quiet and pondered the conundrum.

I looked at J. "You seem anxious; what are you thinking right now?"

J looked down at the floor and said, in a barely audible whisper, "I'm wrestling with the possibility that you might be correct."

"I don't think we should do anything as yet, since you yourself harbor doubts, which I do think is a sign of progress."

J merely nodded at this, albeit with a something of a defeated expression creeping across his face.

"You should take a positive attitude towards this. You may, or may not, have this power to alter printed text, but just look at your recent work. The re-emergence of your revisionist notion has not hampered your ability to function at a superb level in your career, unlike what happened to your work when you were taking the stronger doses of the medications I had initially prescribed. Truly, I think you should be feeling better about yourself right now and try not to be so hard on yourself."

After J left at the end of our session that day, I realized a peculiar thought was bothering me, asking "What if?" What if reality is not as fixed as we all accept it to be? What if I am unwittingly suppressing an odd, but original talent in J, for the sake of standardized medical dogma or, to put it plainly, to keep my own feet firmly on the ground? Had my insisting that J not attempt to demonstrate his alleged Logokinetic ability not been motivated simply to protect him, but rather to protect myself? Was I protecting my patient, myself or both of us? Oddly, a part of me could not answer that question with absolute clarity.

Of course, consistent with the Hippocratic oath: "First, do no harm," I kept telling myself I had to treat J with modified medications to handle his extreme psychological reactions to his fantasy, and remove any internal issues I might have from the equation. Yes, of course, I would do nothing that might actually deepen or strengthen his Revisionist fantasy by encouraging J's desire to try to actualize that belief through physical demonstration. I knew this was naturally the correct and prudent course of treatment any other professional in my field would advocate; naturally I was doing the right thing in my capacity as J's psychiatrist—so why did that nagging "What if" still linger in my thoughts?

Indeed, I would adhere to the treatment plan we'd been following, but the thought—a temptation, if I am to be perfectly honest with myself—kept recurring to me that maybe, just maybe I should let J attempt to prove his Logokenetic ability. If he couldn't alter printed text mentally, the obvious fact that J's so-called ability had been just a delusion all along would be confirmed. But on the other hand, what if J could somehow defy the laws of Physics and demonstrate his alleged Logokinetic abilities? If I can claim to be a scientist as well as a physician, shouldn't I explore every avenue to determine whether J is on to something pertaining to the capacities of the human mind?

Even though we like to think reality is something fixed and immutable, each one of us reacts to reality in highly subjective ways. Recently, my son-in-law, Isaac, showed me an article in *The Journal of Psychiatry* about the potential malleability of perceptions among individual family members. The author of the article, Dr. Michaelmas, argued that individual members of each family did not experience their relationships with their parents or their siblings in the same way. Each family member experienced their family dynamics in truly individual ways and not in a uniform manner as had been long assumed by family therapists. Dr. Michaelmas pointed out how one sibling he encountered in his family practice regarded their father as a man of depth, fun-loving and wonderful company, while another looked at the same father as irritatingly superficial and lacking any genuine interest in who they were as persons. Michaelmas argued in the article that both perceptions should be viewed as perfectly valid given the different psychologies of the two siblings.

The article made me reflect on my own family's dynamics. My eldest son, Joshua, seemed to admire me, inasmuch as he wanted to emulate me and follow a similar career path. However, my younger son, Abram, far from admiring me, appeared to be off in his own world, fascinated as he was with his literally magical thinking, despite my adamant opposition to his interest in magic, which I maintained was illogical.

Indeed, I had often wondered over the years, with no small amount of guilt, whether my rigid negative responses to my own son Abram's readiness to accede to alternate views of reality had pushed him away from me and, in fact, even led to his own ultimate disappearing act, perhaps even damaging his life permanently. Now, oddly, all these years later, J appears in my office, reviving precisely the same struggle I had with my son, Abram. Had J entered my office for a reason? Might he be an opportunity not to repeat the mistakes I made with Abram and, somehow, redeem myself, even if, sadly, it will never bring Abram back to me?

As J's sessions proceeded, while I internally harbored my own doubts as to the nature of our shared perceptions of reality, so far as J was concerned, I maintained that caution was for the best. And so I stuck to my plan of doing nothing for the time being, of doing nothing to encourage J's belief in his Logokenetic abilities.

This plan was thrown into question the very next week, however, when J arrived late to his 2 P.M. appointment. Now, as J had never once been late to any of his prior appointments, I pointed this out to him.

"I'm sorry, Doc., but we spoke of this last session and agreed to change our time to 2:10 P.M. this Wednesday I know we discussed and confirmed it. Don't you remember?"

"I'm sorry, but I recall no such thing."

"Go ahead then, check what's written in your appointment book," J challenged me, with an odd smile playing on his lips.

I looked at my appointment calendar. And, there it was: 2:10 pm, this Wednesday. Yet I had no memory of writing such a time or modifying our normal appointment time. I swore I thought I had written 2 P.M. as usual. When I reiterated this, J let his smile spread wide on his face and merely winked at me.

28.
Joshua Weiss's Senior Year Report Card.
Greensfarm Academy

Report Card: Grade 12

Joshua Weiss

Semester Report: June 10, 1995

Student Grade A
Address 9 Willowbrook Lane
Telephone 203-864-1299
Head Master: Lawrence Tisman

Classes Missed: 0

Times Late: 0

Works Independently: Yes, very well but perhaps too isolated

Teamwork: As noted. A bit of a loner

Organization/Work Habits: Excellent

Homework: Excellent

Initiative: Excellent

Courses

English 407 (Advanced Placement)
Biology 412 (Advanced Placement)
Mathematics 467 (Advanced Placement)
History 406
Chemistry 402

Attendance: Excellent	Grade	Comments
Report Period: January-June 1985 Course Title: Analytical Literature Course Code: ENG407 Instructor: Mr. Henry Smythe	A (E)	Superb, fine grasp of material. He keeps to himself.
Course Title: Studies in Microbiology Course Code: BIO412 Instructor: Mr. Delmore Simpson	A+ (E)	Excellent work, fine Lab work Mr. Weiss is fine student.
Course Title: Calculus and Trigonometry Course Code: MTH467 Instructor: Mr. Larry Gittleman	A (E)	As usual, Mr. Weiss has done top job. He is bright and promising.
Course Title: Contemporary European History Course Code: HIS406 Instructor: Mr. Trevor James	A (E)	Mr. Weiss offers excellent writing and good observations on subject matter. Only deficit: moodiness.
Course Title: Principles of Chemical Analyses Course Code: CHM402 Instructor: Mr. Harry Chelmnitz	A+ (E)	Does excellently, but works best alone. Needs to develop team skills.

Learning Skills
E = Excellent, G = Good
S = Satisfactory
N = Needs Improvement

29.
Letter to Zach re. Joshua's Death

Chief of Westport Police, John O'Malley

Dear Zach,

As you've been a family friend, golf buddy and wonderful part of our community for years, I'm writing you confidentially about the horrific loss to your family and our town of your eldest son, Joshua.

I'm sorry to tell you the Coroner found your son's blood-alcohol level was twice the normal limit for driving, which no doubt contributed to his fatal car crash. However, in consideration of our friendship and my deepest respect for you and my sympathy for you and your family in your time of grief, I have spoken with the Coroner and want to assure you that this information won't be shared with the public or the local papers such as *The Town Crier* or the *Westport Daily*.

Sending you and your family my most heartfelt condolences,

John

30.
Esther Weiss's Day Planner

May 22, 1995

<u>May 22, Tuesday</u>

Zach:

1. Have Zach see if Inez has prepared food for sitting Shiva for Joshua.
2. Remind Zach to speak with Rabbi about his Eulogy.
3. Lay out yarmulkah, black suit on bed.

Myself:

1. Wear white blouse with black dress.
2. Have Inez get linens and plates ready for reception.
3. Deep breathing, meditation, stay calm.

Joshua:

1. Have Inez change sheets on his bed and air out room.
2. See if photo shop can repair those damaged photos of Josh.

Abram:

1. Lay out his Brooks Brothers dark suit and yamalkah.

Sara:

1. Lay out her navy-blue dress from her suit case. Looks better than black one she wants to wear.

31.
The Diary of Isaac Himmelfarb

June 17, 2018

After my clear inability as a husband to help my wife and, despite all the love I have for Sara, that night last week when I found Sara back in her childhood bedroom drunk made me realize assistance could only come from a third-party, objective source. Sara has now been doing daily sessions the past three days with a female colleague of mine, Dr. Rachel Jacobs, with whom Sara seems to be gradually heading or, at least, moving toward a more stable condition.

In the meantime, resisting my own inclination to feel like a failure as a husband in the face of my inability to help Sara on my own (despite my sense of knowing her better than anyone in the world and my being a psychiatric professional), I have been burying myself in reviewing Zach's papers.

Outside of my practice, sensing Sara's desire for "alone-time," as she puts it, I've even been lingering many nights in Zach's study looking at all the boxes containing articles, monographs and professional journals. The papers and monographs, of course, need to go to some university library, perhaps the Widener at Harvard, which was after all Zach's Alma Mater, so I'll try them first. Although given the notoriety of the Revisionist business, Zach's documents pertaining to that case I feel are best kept private.

In the last set of notes I found that Zach wrote about the case of J, he'd written how I'd given him that article by Dr. Michaelmas about family dynamics, which I hadn't thought of in years, but then recalled how, at the time, I'd thought Zach might find the article insightful about his own family dynamics, although I offered it to him ostensibly as being relevant to the peculiar case of his patient J and J's issues with his own deceased father. It had never occurred to me when I handed that article to Zach that it might lead him to link Abram and J in his own thoughts.

As I read and reread Zach's documents pertaining to the case of his career-ending patient J, it seems I can read between the lines how Zach was wrestling with the question: How does one harmonize or indeed interact with ghosts? They reside within our minds and have no existence apart from us. Yet, they can interact with some of us as if living beings or even via other actual living beings. But the relationship with these ghosts shifts and changes as different memories are invoked with a look at a book or some document that relates to that individual.

As I review his papers and documents, Zach takes on different forms in my mind. From an examination of the notes on his sessions with patients, one moment he's the brilliant analyst, dissecting human motivations. The next moment, when I look at that mad, final letter Abram wrote to Zach, I see him as the stubborn dogmatist father whose absolute resistance to his son's inclination toward mysticism drove Abram to a perilous edge. In Zach's blind determination to have Abram fit into a rational slot in the family unit, Zach takes on the menacing guise of the all-powerful patriarch who can sacrifice his son on the altar of psychiatric dogma, a bit like Abraham with my namesake, Isaac—only in Abram's case no ram showed up to take his place—at least not until J showed up, but then it was sadly too late to save Abram.

Then, it hit me; Zach had a multitude of family relationships he was trying to harmonize while I only have my relationship with Sara and, between us, both of us have our own distinct and shared ghosts. Indeed, I remain haunted by a ghost: my father who committed suicide, while Sara, on the other hand, has the ghost of her dead brother Joshua (as well as the quasi-ghost of her missing brother Abram), and now the ghost of her father, Zach. And as something shared, at the same time, somehow hovering like a dangerous bridge between us, Sara and I also have the most intense ghost of all in our own nameless, lost child.

32.
Excerpt from The Revisionist: A Case of Logokinesis Mania

Dr. Zachary Weiss

There was a disturbing sequel to the incident about the schedule mix-up: J had insisted we were to meet at 2:10 P.M. rather than our usual time, 2 P.M. As I've already noted, when I looked at the calendar, it definitely did appear that I had written 2:10 P.M., although I couldn't recall any such time change. Again, as I've already noted, after drawing my attention to the time in my calendar, J let a broad smile spread across his face and merely winked at me. Now it strikes me that he perhaps felt this time change somehow demonstrated this gift he claimed to have for physically altering text by mental willpower. After he left that day, and after I'd finished responding to an email and was waiting for my next appointment, I couldn't resist looking again at my calendar: J's appointment time for the session at that point read 2 P.M., as I had insisted it was all along.

I was, of course, puzzled, but more than that, I wondered if I now had to entertain the idea that there might be something tangible to J's belief in his ability to alter printed text mentally, albeit perhaps limited in duration. How could I not?

Of course, I know that in the mainstream psychiatrists are often referred to in a reductive and rather insulting way as "shrinks," as if we are shrinking our patients' minds or psyches or, at the least, altering them. In truth, I must confess, from a certain point of view, there is some merit to the notion that psychoanalysis does involve, in the process of what Freud called "the talking cure," the analyst facilitating a change in the patient's psyche, albeit a healthy change. But my work with J made me wonder if this normal analyst/patient dynamic was being challenged.

Was J trying to turn the tables on me? Was J attempting to facilitate a change in my psyche rather than the other, normal, way around? Was I now in a situation where my patient was playing at changing my psyche? And, if he was, what if J were succeeding?

On the other hand (as I kept reminding myself I had to believe), if J's alleged power of Logokinesis could be dismissed as mere delusion, might it be that J was somehow an extraordinary hypnotist? Might J be such an amazing hypnotist that he could convince a person—even a trained professional, such as myself, educated by years of experience at discerning the difference between what was real and what wasn't—into blurring the line separating reality from delusion?

Lately, I've caught myself connecting J and my poor son, Abram, in my thoughts. Had I been too rigid in my rejection of my own son's early belief in magic? Shouldn't I have humored Abram when his interest first arose and let him work it through as he got older? If I had, maybe he would have realized that professional magicians use clever legerdemain tricks, like misdirection, to fool an audience into believing, for a moment, that their tricks are real—but magicians themselves never actually believe their own tricks are real. Might both my son and J share the bizarre case of resembling something like quasi-magicians who somehow suffered in the belief that their own tricks were real? At least, Abram, after his breakdown, seems to have managed to create his own reality after all. But hadn't J, after his father's death, done precisely the same thing?

Sadly, it's too late for me to save my own son, Abram, or to go back in time and be less rigid with him; however, it just might not be too late to help J—though I must be careful not to let myself share J's own delusions, which he clearly wants me to do.

On the one hand, I must be careful not to insist that J's belief in his mental powers should be pigeonholed within some rigid psychiatric category such as psychosis. I have to tread carefully since, as early as our first session, I observed J's inclination to become very agitated rapidly when discussing his Logokenesis mania. Yet, for the life of me, the longer I work with this patient, the more intensely curious I have become—even to the point of entertaining possibilities I heretofore would have adamantly dismissed as rubbish—I now often have difficulty sleeping and find myself listening less closely to my other patients than I ever have before in my entire career.

At our next session, which happened coincidentally to occur just after I had been rereading Freud's *The Interpretation of Dreams* for background on a paper I was writing about the correlation of dreams to the creative process before my session with J, I had absentmindedly left the book on my desk when J entered.

As he sat down, he immediately noticed the book on my desk, excitedly pointed to it and said: "I know that book, *Basic Writings of Sigmund Freud.* That's the Modern Library edition. I recall a passage in *The Interpretation of Dreams*, right on page 223, that's always annoyed me because it's deliberately been translated into archaic English. The lines that bother me on that page are from a poem. I recall the translation reads: 'The best that thou canst know thou mayst not tell to boys.' I hate that sort of translating. It sounds so pretentious! It ought to read naturally, such as: 'The best you can know, you can't tell to children.'"

Before I could look up the passage, there was a knock on my door. It was the building superintendent. He apologized for disturbing me but had to tell me that one of the pipes had burst in the basement and that the water would have to be shut off in the building. After the superintendent left, J and I finished our session. It was fairly unremarkable. J had complained that an older woman in his office had been promoted to a senior editorial position over him, which he resented, yet, despite his frustration with her promotion, he confessed he still found this older woman extremely attractive—even if he felt she'd robbed him of a job that should've been his and there was a twenty-year age difference between them. He went on to admit that he often found himself distracted by her at work, sometimes could not resist staring at her, especially when she came into the office wearing a Chanel suit, and J even confessed he'd had sexual fantasies involving her.

When I suggested a possible resemblance between his co-worker and his mother, J insisted angrily that my suggestion was absurd, even obscene, and had nothing whatsoever to do with his attraction to the older woman in his office. The session thus ended on a bit of a bad note, with J frowning as he quickly left my office.

A few minutes after J was gone, I recalled how our session had begun and took the book on Freud from my desk and turned to page 223. What I saw there was that the text J had spoken of at the start of our session now read exactly as J said it should, in modern English, not the archaic variety that I knew had been there before. It now read, 'The best you can know, you can't tell to children.' I thought: He really did it!

First the calendar, now this: yet again, I could not resist the feeling that J was turning the tables on me—rather than me facilitating a positive change in my patient's psyche, J was challenging a part of the very foundation of my own psyche.

As I read and reread J's modern translation in Freud's book on my desk, appearing as undeniably as it did in black and white print on the page, I saw another proof that there was either something to J's claim that he could actually re-edit text mentally, or that he was a master hypnotist, or that I was losing my own grip on reality.

As I drove home after finishing with my last patient that day (whose complaints about her husband's infidelities I barely heard and was unable to respond to beyond offering her an occasional nod), I had the Freud book from my office in my briefcase lying on the passenger seat beside me, while my thoughts were racing along with the engine of my car. As soon as I got home, I rushed into my office, opened my briefcase, took out the Freud book, and opened it on my desk to page 223.

Now, here on my desk at home, in the exact same book I'd perused with such astonishment in my office, I found the text on page 223 had reverted back to the archaic English that had originally been there: "The best that thou canst know thou mayst not tell to boys." Tentatively, I concluded that either whatever power J had was only temporary in duration, like my calendar. Then I wondered whether this might be an incredible discovery, suggesting that the human mind had hidden abilities we had no idea existed except in the realm of fiction. I even could not resist thinking of the professional recognition I might receive if J's case warranted a new entry identifying Logokinesis Mania in the next DSM V and crediting me with the discovery of this new and singular mania.

But later, over dinner, my thoughts consumed me so intensely that I was unable to speak with Esther. I hardly touched the food on my plate and found myself worrying that I was now sharing my patient's delusion. Had J won in the game of turning the tables or had I made a genuine discovery of an actual new mania—I had to figure out which it was.

Even after dinner, I continued wrestling the rest of the night with the uncertainty J's case presented to me. Indeed, mulling over the possibilities kept me up all night.

33.
Private Report on Abram Weiss Initiated by His Father, Dr. Zachary Weiss

Spireman's Confidential Investigations

Spireman & McPhail, LLM.
528 East 48th Street, suite 5B
New York, NY 10218
(212) 472-8463
SpiremanNyc@msn.com

Case # A507b, Final Report # 5. October 24, 2011

Intra-Office Memorandum re. Investigation of Abram Weiss

This investigation's subject, Abram Weiss, the son of our client, Dr. Zachary Weiss, initially went missing after dropping out of Harvard University in 2002. Although our client conveyed to us that he had hired multiple different Private Investigators over the past eight years, starting immediately after the initial disappearance of his son, none of the other investigators had succeeded in locating subject. However, our investigation, after exhaustive tracking and research, did locate our client's son.

Our detectives assigned to pin down the exact whereabouts of Abram Weiss, the son of our client, Dr. Zachary Weiss, discovered that Abram had, at some point, changed his name to Magnus Pater and established himself as the head of a cult religion of his own creation. Our investigation further revealed that Abram/Magnus had organized a commune for his followers located at Wild Brush Ranch just outside of Modesto, California 90634. This commune houses approximately 150 of the followers Abram/Magnus Pater has recruited to his cult and has a single phone number: (914) 634-6660.

Calling themselves the Society of the Divine Receptor, our investigation further found that Abram's followers claim that our client's son, their leader, whom they identify as Magnus Pater, receives divine messages from a quartet of sacred sages who are Moses, Jesus Christ, the Buddha and a mysterious fourth spirit the cult refers to only as the Spectral Handler.

This so-called new religion itself is mainly composed of an assortment of New Age ideas about channeling spiritual energy through special chants, while also entertaining a peculiar apocalyptic vision of a final confrontation between the forces of good and evil, which their leader (our client's son), maintains will eventually take place in Los Angeles.

After we apprised our client, Dr. Zachary Weiss, of his son's precise whereabouts and the means to contact him, we learned through our lead investigator that our client later shared with him that he had called his son, Abram/Magnus, but our client's efforts to talk with his son, after so many years of not knowing where he was, apparently were not met with a positive response. Indeed, in a moment of unusual candor regarding the failed father-son reconnect our client had so desperately hoped for, Dr. Weiss related that his son refused to talk to his father, saying only that he, Magnus, now superseded his "former father" in all spiritual matters and felt any "earthly connection" between them was of no consequence and merely an annoyance, distracting Magnus from the important work his followers relied on him to be doing.

After this, Dr. Zachary Weiss thanked us for locating his son, but informed us that he no longer required our services. This report serves as our intra-office conclusion of this investigation.

Travel expenses and other ancillary costs incurred in the course of this case have been sent with our final bill for services rendered to the client.

35.
Zachary Weiss's Note Scribbled at Home, 3 A.M. re: Case of J

Tonight, as I tossed and turned in bed, trying not to wake up Esther but myself unable to sleep, a thought struck me so powerfully I had to get out of bed and write it down so I won't forget it myself:

What if all my own internal wrestling that has arisen since working with J has been the result of an entirely rational oversight? As a trained MD, albeit one specializing in the field of psychiatry, might my recent perceptions in the cases of both my calendar and my book of Freud have nothing to do with J?. Might it just as possibly be a mere coincidence that these odd or altering perceptions occurred while having J as a patient, yet these experiences I've had with both perceptions could actually be symptoms of the earliest stage or onset of Alzheimer's or some other neurological disorder?

As all analysts undergo their own analysis, I underwent analysis with my mentor, the brilliant doctor Jacob Auerbach, who always maintained that nothing should be ruled out. Consistent with his credo and the training I received from him, no doubt I should make an appointment with a neurologist ASAP.

BOOK TWO

Wherein the narrative departs from its confinement to the contents of documents found in the boxes in Zach's home office and Isaac's diary entries, and offers additional documents that arose as a result of the revelation that Isaac's brother-in-law, Abram, was alive and active in Modesto, California.

1.
Letter to Magnus Pater, né Abram Weiss

Isaac A. Himmelfarb, M.D.
Clinical Psychiatrist
Specialist in Child Psychology
4 East 89th Street
New York, NY 10028
Phone: (212) 347-5678
E-mail: Ishim@msn.com

June 20, 2018

Dear Magnus,
Sadly, I am writing this letter to you, after so many years of our not being in touch, with unhappy news I wish I didn't have to convey to you or, at least, had been able to get to you earlier. It is with great sorrow that I must inform you of your father's passing. Specifically, he died in the early hours of May 30th. I truly regret and apologize for not contacting you sooner. The problem was I did not have your current address and discovered it only today.

Sara and I were at your father's bedside just before he died. Due to the cancer your father was fighting for so long, he looked much older than his sixty years, more like a bald Methuselah with a short beard rather than the long, luxuriant ones the Patriarchs wore in those illustrated Bible stories we read in Hebrew school when we were boys.

Despite the late hour, as the end was imminent, we waited in chairs beside your father's bed. At 2 A.M., your father passed away. The funeral was held May 31st. Both Sara and I are so sorry you weren't able to be there.

Yours truly,
Isaac

2.
Letter from Magnus Pater, né Abram Weiss

The Society of the Divine Receptor
Wild Brush Ranch
Modesto, CA 90634
Phone: (914) 634-6660
Fax: (914) 634-6661
Website: wwwIAMIT.com

His Serene Receptor,
Seven Times Blessed
By the Kisses of Moses,
The Embraces of Jesus
And the Caresses of Buddha,
Solidified by the Spectral Handler
Magnus Pater Sends Greetings
To You, Dr. Isaac Himmelfarb,
on this day, June 28, 2018,

We have read your missive with sadness concerning the passing of that man who in my former life I had hailed as father. It was always grievous to our *magnum cor* that he never accepted my divine mission. But, the conflicts between fathers and those they claim to be their children must not be unknown to you, dear doctor, given your profession as child psychiatrist?

Yet, we write to you not only to return to the territory

of our former so-called father, but to discover if our former father had made mention of a case in which a young man had come to him claiming to have the power to alter physically printed text.

We have long held all material representations in this world set down to communicate mortal ideas in such things as books are but illusion, yet we never saw actual proof of this before an unusual young man recently arrived at our Order seeking comfort.

In our conversations he told us how he tried to receive psychiatric assistance or clarity for what he regarded as a gift, but which the doctor he met with initially identified in a reductive manner as a "problem." Eventually, after extensive talks with this unusual young man, we realized his doctor was our former father. This troubled soul indicated that his association with our former father was a principal cause for the latter's retirement from his profession.

Therefore, we entreat you to write us in greater detail as to any information and documents you can provide in regards to the case of this unusual young man and tortured soul who now resides in our community and was known as "the Revisionist."

Again, any documents you might send me that my former father might have penned pertaining to the so-called "revisionist" would be greatly appreciated and specifically helpful so that we might be able to communicate this information with Moses, Jesus and Buddha that they may advise us how best to proceed with the treatment of this case and have it articulated by the Spectral Handler.

Finally, what also intrigues us is that this young man has made claim that it was his case and the unsuccessful resolution of it that led to our former father's premature retirement. So, for all these reasons, any documents our former father may have left concerning this man would be greatly welcomed by us, if you could kindly forward them to this, our earthly address. Lastly, we would, of course, also be delighted to hear news concerning our former sister, Sara, as well as our former mother, Esther.

ARTICULATED BY THE GRACE OF
the SPECTRAL HANDLER,
Magnus Pater

3.
The Diary of Isaac Himmelfarb

July 3, 2018

It breaks my heart that my childhood friend and brother-in-law, Abram, seems to have integrated his psychosis into a distinct, religious personality where he regards himself as a divine figure. Those caught in such a psychosis suffer as their ego is magnified into a truly grotesque megalomania. He always wanted magic to be real as a boy and now, sadly it seems, as a psychotic adult he's achieved his dream and even gathered a large number of followers to his cult.

It's interesting that, in Abram's mind, I suspect Zach failed to help him by not responding to Abram's clearly deranged last letter to his father. Now that J has ended up with Abram in his commune, it's natural that Abram, once finding out about Zach's passing, would want background information on his latest convert, particularly given his connection to Zach.

But that's a problem. J was Zach's patient and I'm the custodian of Zach's papers. Abram's letter was clearly written by a man who is profoundly disturbed mentally. Thus, it would be irresponsible of me as a doctor to entrust Zach's papers about J to a psychotic, even if he is Zach's son. Even if Abram was my childhood friend—this Magnus is no longer the Abram I knew.

Beyond violating doctor-patient confidentiality between J and Zach, given the evidence of psychosis in Abram's letter, I just can't responsibly let Abram know about the notes and the unfinished monograph Zach wrote about J. As much as I hate to lie to Abram, fondly recalling our shared childhood, I must, otherwise I'd be breaking both doctor-patient confidentiality, and the very opening of the Hippocratic Oath, "First, do no harm." I can't even begin to imagine how two mentally disturbed people such as Abram/Magnus and J might react to what Zach wrote. No, Zach's papers on J must stay top secret from Abram. This is one occasion where the truth would be worse than a lie.

My G-d, it just struck me—not only must I withhold the truth from Abram and J, but also I must withhold the truth from my wife, Sara, by not letting her know that I am in touch with her brother. Although Abram may be her brother, and so a part of me does feel I should let her know I've located him and am, in fact, corresponding with him, a much bigger part of me is scared of letting Sara know the truth inasmuch as, if she were to get in touch with Abram, I've no doubt she would quickly discern that her brother is sadly in a psychotic state. I'm certain that would only compound the double depression she is already struggling with over the recent death of her father and the miscarriage of our child.

It was bad enough, years ago, when she saw Abram spiral downhill into his initial stage of psychosis at Harvard. For her to learn of his current condition today, given her emotionally fragile state, could have horrific repercussions. It also strikes me now that if Sara were to learn that her father knew, from the detective's report, exactly where her brother was for so long and never shared that information with her, poor Sara would be, at the same time, both furious with her father, Zach, while also still wrestling with her grief and sense of loss from his recent death. Yes, once again, it does seem there are multiple occasions where the truth can be worse than a lie.

4.
Letter to Magnus Pater, né Abram Weiss

Isaac A. Himmelfarb, M.D.
Clinical Psychiatrist,
Specialist in Child Psychology
4 East 89th Street
New York, NY 10028
Phone: (212) 347-5678
E-mail: Ishim@msn.com

July 5, 2018

Dear Magnus,
Per your request in your letter for news as to your mother and sister, I am so sorry to have to tell you by letter that Sara has been combatting depression since your father passed away and your mother, Esther, is now in the early stages of Alzheimer's. Again, I'm sorry you had to find this out by letter.

Beyond sad family news, I must confess I was amazed to find out via your letter that you are taking care of your father's last patient, the so-called Revisionist. I would welcome hearing what your assessment is of this man and also to arrange a chance for me to meet him. It would really mean a lot to me. In response to your request, I'm sorry to tell you that, despite searching your father's papers, I cannot find any documents he wrote about the Revisionist case at all.

As far as what your father felt about the Revisionist, given the complete absence of any documents written by your father pertaining to this man, I can only speculate as to how your father did or did not view this his last patient. Of course, with nothing to go on, such guesswork by me regarding his last patient would, I think, be useless to either of us. Only once did he speak to me in passing of the Revisionist and that was when he asked me not to mention this patient to Sara as he wanted to spare her any more embarrassment or upset over the case that led to his retirement. He thought she was upset enough by the spreading of his cancer.

Yours truly,
Isaac

5.
Letter from Magnus Pater, né Abram Weiss

The Society of the Divine Receptor
Wild Brush Ranch
Modesto, CA 90634
Phone: (914) 634-6660
Fax: (914) 634-6661
Website: WWWIAMIT.com

His Serene Receptor,
Seven Times Blessed
By the Kisses of Moses,
The Embraces of Jesus
And the Caresses of Buddha,
Solidified by the Spectral Handler
Magnus Pater Sends Greetings
To You, Dr. Isaac Himmelfarb,
on this day, July 10, 2018.

As to your report on my former sister and former mother, I am saddened. However, concerning our former mother, Esther, do not be concerned as what this world calls Alzheimer's the Lord Buddha has assured us leaves our former mother much happier, in a childlike state, liberated from the burdens of memory. Still, though I must express my gratitude for your writing, in my communications with Moses, Jesus and the Lord Buddha, with the insight of the Spectral Handler, I found they felt you were holding back or unwilling to share information with us about the so-called "Revisionist" Case.

We know through divine whispering that our former sister, Sara, must be grievously afflicted as we have seen her through the spectral lens turning to alcoholic beverages and solace through different varieties of pharmaceuticals, an evil which we are dedicated to weaning off all those seeking our aid.

Let us reassure you that no matter how unusual our beliefs may appear to the alien world, we want only what is best for our former sister and former mother, as well as this man who came to us in need.

Please know that given the divine status of our guides, they would not intrude themselves on the privacy of others unless given permission. What this means is that they will not read our former father's papers if you do not voluntarily send those documents my former father wrote, which the Spectral Handler has informed us that you possess. No matter how serious the situation is for this man whom our former father failed to "cure," our celestial communicants will not assist us unless we receive a copy of my former father's documents from you.

If it will give you a measure of confidence that we are already familiar with much of the case, we can tell you some of its particulars as related to us by this young man. We hasten to reassure you that we received his consent to do so since he agreed to place his care in our hands. We enclose, in a sealed envelope, his statement of consent to assure you of our good will.

This young man was a book editor for a company called Banner Books in New York City. He told us he had enjoyed reading and editing books since his childhood. He said everything was going well until he became obsessed with Kafka's *Metamorphosis*. He was particularly anxious to discover into what form of insect the hero of that story, Gregor Samsa, was transformed. Apparently, after a strange dream involving a dung beetle, he claimed the printed text of his translation of the work had actually changed to read that Mr. Samsa was changed into a dung beetle rather than an enormous insect as before. He said that our former father's efforts to "cure" him were fleeting and ended in failure.

We felt that this unique, remarkable and anguished man was led to us through years of suffering because of a psychic affinity between us. Even though he did not know our connection to our former father, our young man sensed it for he was strongly drawn to travel westward toward us after leaving our former father's care. Indeed, the actual presence of this young man among us remains a proof of this.

So, once again, we request you provide us with our former father's written documents concerning this man's case if you hope to be able to visit us as our guest and, perhaps, meet this man.

ARTICULATED BY THE GRACE OF
the SPECTRAL HANDLER,
Magnus Pater

6.
Enclosure with Letter from Magnus Pater, né Abram Weiss, Determined to Be from J of the Revisionist Case

To Whom It May Concern:
I implore that you give my Grand Receptor, Magnus Pater, all the help he may need in gathering information concerning my gift or malady (depending on whom you ask) so that he might receive the inspiration he needs from his celestial guides to help me.

I assert that I am of sound mind and I give this permission of my own free will.

The one the world knew as Wilfred Pierce,
Wilfred Pierce,
now *Cygnus*

7.
The Diary of Isaac Himmelfarb

7/15/18

Damn! Abram does indeed seem to be psychotic, but not stupid. It's as if (despite his claims as to what the spirits have told him) he knows intuitively that I was lying when I asserted that Zach left behind no papers on the Revisionist Case. Yet, I'm still firmly resolved that neither Abram nor J can ever see these documents. I guess in my next letter to Abram, I'm going to have to be more creative—come up with some story he'll buy, some contrived explanation I need to create to sell him on the unavailability of any papers from his father on the Revisionist. But, hell, I'm no creative writer; I'm a psychiatrist. Still, it seems this situation demands the creation of a credible story, a bit of fiction that I must present as fact.

Perhaps, since it's a fact Zach was shattered by the outcome of the Revisionist business, I'll start by confessing to Abram that it is true that, at some point, the documents he's seeking did exist, but then I'll have to offer him some sort of fictional explanation as to why those documents are now gone. But what can I say? I can't just say they were carried off by the wind or some such transparent lie. I need a truly decent and believable explanation for the disappearance of these documents—but what the hell might that be? I don't know. Of course, I can apologize for not telling Abram everything before, but what follows my apology must be my now telling him the "truth"—whatever I decide it to be—to explain why there's nothing to send him.

It just struck me: I'll be acting like J—I'll be revising reality to fit the outcome I desire—Abram's acceptance that the Revisionist Case files are gone. J's belief, that he could alter printed text by mental willpower, is called psychosis, but won't my describing false events also be my own altering of reality? Indeed, Abram has constructed his own reality on the basis of his religious psychosis. J found his own delusional means of manipulating reality with his mind. But, here I am, seeking to do essentially the same thing as both of them in my correspondence with Abram. Yet, while they are both psychotics, my own tinkering with reality I regard as not remotely psychotic, but merely my exercising what the world regards as "discretion." Although, in fairness to myself: I can create a false narrative and step out of it while Abram and J are hopelessly entangled in theirs.

8.
Excerpt from *The Revisionist: A Case of Logokinesis Mania*

Dr. Zachary Weiss

Now comes the moment of truth. I've been to my neurologist to ensure that my experiences of text alteration with J are not the result of a physiological condition. The results of the tests gave me a clean bill of health: the MRI showed I was fine. This means (unless I myself am losing my grip on reality by embracing the delusions of my patient) I'm on the verge of making a scientific discovery that would have radical implications of how the human brain perceives and interprets reality. This would go beyond Heisenberg's Uncertainty Principle, where what we observe is subtly altered by the very act of observation. If J can physically alter printed text through mental willpower, this effect wouldn't be subtle, it would be obvious to all.

After the neurologist gave me a clean bill of health, I decided to reverse my earlier reluctance to let J attempt to demonstrate his Logokinesis, so much so that at our next session, as soon as J arrived at my office, I said to him, "I've been considering your repeated requests in our past sessions to demonstrate this ability you believe you have to alter printed text with your mind, which I've felt was inappropriate to encourage before, but now I have decided, in the interests of science, as well as your treatment, to offer you the opportunity to demonstrate this ability you've maintained you have."

J could hardly contain his own excitement. "Thank you, Doctor, for giving me this chance to prove to you that I can alter printed text. But, if I demonstrate this ability to you, what do you think it could mean? I know with absolute certainty I have this ability, and now I will be happy to prove it to you, but I've always been at a loss to understand what my ability signifies or where it leaves me as to my place in the world at large?"

"I certainly don't want to jump to conclusions, but, it's possible that you could be the harbinger of the next stage of human evolution. Even though evolution is usually a very slow business, taking thousands of years to emerge, there are instances where evolution leaps forward in a radical burst in various species. You could be the first to manifest what might be one of the most profound stages of evolution itself. But, enough theorizing, if you can indeed prove you have this ability, we can work together in our sessions here to resolve the question of how or where this locates you in the world at large. But first things first, let's get to work. Pick any book in my library and let's see what you can do."

"Fair enough." J then perused my books and pulled out a slim paperback volume I had of Jung's famous essay on synchronicity. J looked at the autobiographical summary of Jung's life on the first page and mulled it over, nodding his head a few times. "Here, Doctor, I think you'll find this amusing."

I looked at the text. It now read: "Carl Jung was born in Brooklyn, New York in 1875 and attended Harvard University where he was expelled for urinating on the statue of John Harvard after getting drunk at a frat party. In shame, he left the US and settled in Switzerland where he finished his education. He met and, for a time, was a disciple of Sigmund Freud. They later fell out, both over Freud's theory of sexuality and the fact that Jung beat Freud in arm wrestling."

I couldn't help but laugh out loud. "This is amazing and truly funny at the same time. Do you see any other books you wish to try your gift out on?"

"Yes, I noticed you had a volume of Wordsworth's poetry. Here, look at one of his most famous lines."

J held the book open to the page he wanted me to see. Instead of the famous opening, "I wandered lonely as a cloud," it now read, "I wandered lonely as a dung beetle."

I couldn't help but stare at J in amazement. Even though based on my observations of J's past efforts, I had expected these revisions to last only for a short period of time, my mind started racing with thoughts as to how I might, under more controlled conditions, arrange to demonstrate J's Logokinetic abilities concretely to the world and, in so doing, arrive at the capstone to my career: a truly great scientific discovery which would alter the very course of the study of human physiology (and psychology) in the years to come.

9.
Transcript of Message Left on Dr. Himmelfarb's Answering Machine

July 16, 2018

Phone Message:
Sweetie, it's Sara. I hate to bother you at your office when you're working, but I have to tell you it seems my mom's Alzheimer's is getting worse. I just found in her dresser drawer her latest day planner page. It just doesn't make any sense at all. She still has entries for Joshua, Abram and Dad—it's as though she's in some sort of crazy time warp where she thinks they are all still at home or she thinks me, Joshua and Abram are still kids.

I know you've been worried about me, Isaac, and it's true I've not been myself since we lost both my dad and our baby, but now, on top of everything else, as if I'm not already overwhelmed enough as it is, it seems my mom's really losing it bigtime!

I knew she reacted to Joshua's death years ago in a weird way, which might have been an early indication of her already being a bit unstable back then. I remember how she never acknowledged Joshua was gone, despite being at the funeral, the *shiva* and the unveiling of his tombstone a year later. Maybe you remember how distracted she seemed. But looking at her latest day planner just now, I think she's lost it on a far more intense level than ever before and I feel so sad for Mom, as well as feeling horribly alone myself—like my whole family is gone, except for you.

Oh Isaac, I'm so sorry to bother you and I don't mean to upset you, but I'm alone, talking to your machine while watching my mom fading away right in front of me, and I need you, not as a patient, but as your wife. Damn it, Ize, don't reduce me to a case study; I'm your wife. I'm not angry with you. Maybe I'm just angry at life and at having to feel so helpless. Please call me back when you can, Honey. I do love you and am glad you're there for me.

10.
Esther Weiss's Day Planner

July 15, 2018

Zach:
Have suits clean for next week.
Where is Zach hiding? Seems moody last I talked with him. Should I have him talk with Rabbi Jacobs? But Rabbi Jacobs doesn't answer my phone calls? Someone else is using his number. Did I get typing paper for him? I must have.

Myself:
Did I miss the Hadassah meeting? I must ask Sara
Talk to Glenda about dust. Too much dust everywhere.
Count silverware again. One spoon missing, I'm sure of it. Can I trust Glenda?

Joshua:
Have Glenda clean dust balls from under his bed.
See if his suits are properly pressed.
Joshua is coming home soon, have mirrors cleaned.

Abram:
He has to go to Brooks Brothers for fresh clothes.
Check to see if he's left me a phone message from Harvard.
Maybe Zach should call Harvard's student health department about Abram.

Sara:
See if her dorm room has proper security.
Have her <u>find</u> Abram and get him to a barber shop.
Get her to write to me at least once a week about Abram and things in general.

11.
Zachary Weiss's note on patient Pierce, also Ref'd to as J

As an author of many books, treatises, case studies, I've always believed that a word once written down was indelible. One could tear up the paper or erase what one has written so that no one else might read it; yet, even though that word's life might be as brief as a breath, that act of writing on paper was a commitment to permanence. But now, I believe, such commitment is temporal, not permanent. This goes against my old beliefs, yet, I've seen how words written down can change on the page.

After what I saw of J's manipulation of Freud's text and my calendar, I've since conducted tests with J to alter other texts. He again convincingly demonstrated his ability to alter texts with a brief biography of Jung as well as the opening line of a well-known Wordsworth poem. I've already reduced J's meds, but now have taken J off all of his meds entirely. I know this goes against my prior opinion of not humoring what I had previously thought was J's delusion or reducing his meds any further, but I've got to know what's what!

Oh G-d, what if someone ever sees this? Will they think I'm mad as J or unethical for taking J off his meds and entertaining such tests? No matter, screw my colleagues with their cozy suburban practices snoozing through sessions with bored housewives or those know-it-all pill pushers hardly listening to patients as they scribble scrip after scrip for the latest psychotropic meds—I

him if I should call 911. But my question only seemed to irritate him as he angrily said, "No," and insisted, "it's nothing like that at all—just get the hell over here Isaac." After that, I assured him I would get dressed and be at his home shortly. However, as soon as I hung up the phone, I realized that Sara was sitting up in bed by then, fully awake.

Naturally, Sara asked about the phone call and, after I came clean—though I was concerned not to worry her about the odd call from her father—she asked me if she should come as well to see your father. Recalling the obvious heightened agitation in Zach's voice on the phone only moments earlier, I'd no idea how he might appear when I met him face to face and worried that if he was in a bad way emotionally it would only add to Sara's sadness over Zach's deterioration. For this reason, I told your sister that she should not worry and go back to sleep, that I would only be away a short time and that her father had asked not for her, but only me to come over to his place. I can tell you, Sara was not pleased by this at all, but finally accepted it after she made me promise to call her if, after I saw her father, I felt anything serious was wrong.

Once I got to your family's home, I saw the light was on at the front door. I quietly knocked, hoping Zach would be waiting for me in the foyer, so I wouldn't disturb your mom, who I assumed was sleeping. As it happened, my hunch was correct and Zach opened the front door after my first knock, as if he'd been standing there waiting for it. I was immediately struck by the fact that Zach was fully dressed, as if he were about to leave for work: red tie, blue shirt, Harris tweed jacket and chinos. I also couldn't help but notice how loosely his clothes hung on his body. His face was thin, with a greyish pallor. Sadness swept over me seeing how graphically his illness had taken its toll on him.

I asked Zach what was so important that it couldn't wait until daylight. He looked at me with sunken eyes and said, it was something he had to do now before he got too weak to do it later and that it was something that couldn't be done in the light of day. I'd no idea what he meant and said so. In response, your father merely muttered that it was time to revise and erase a specific piece of history. When I asked him what that meant, he ignored my question and simply said, "Look Isaac, are you going to help me or not? If you are, get the lighter fluid for the barbeque out of the garage and then come to my office." When I tried to ask him why on earth he needed lighter fluid, he almost shouted at me (something your father had never done before in all the years I'd known him), "Just get the goddamn lighter fluid!"

Seeing his extremely agitated state, despite fearing there might be some danger in whatever the hell it was he wanted me to help him with, I went to the garage, got the can of lighter fluid and then went to his office where I found him assembling a pile of documents. After noticing me in the doorway of his office, he merely nodded and resumed selecting papers to add to the growing pile on his desk. Having no clue as to just what he was up to, I observed him silently and waited for him to speak.

Finally, smiling with an odd sort of satisfaction, your father announced that we were now ready to revise history, asked me to hand him the can of lighter fluid, and then instructed me to lift the pile of documents from his desk and follow him, which I did. When we'd reached the barbeque in the backyard, he removed the grill, tossed it on the grass, and told me to drop the papers into the pan beneath, which I also did, but not before noting various phrases or words hinting at the content of these documents. I saw just enough to realize that those papers pertained to the so-called Revisionist case. At that moment, it struck me that your father had decided to erase any documentary evidence of the case that had left such a blot on his name and reputation.

As your father sprayed and soaked the papers in lighter fluid until he'd emptied the can, he was laughing to himself in a peculiar, almost hysterical way, as if he'd entirely forgotten I was standing beside him and thought he was alone. In all the years I'd known your father, I'd never heard such laughter from him and never witnessed him in such an agitated state. There we were, standing alone in the backyard, at about 3 A.M. by that point, enveloped in darkness.

Neither of us moved for a moment, then suddenly your father pulled a small box of stick matches from the pocket of his tweed coat. Just as he was about to strike a match, I protested and tried to persuade him not to do it. I told him that he owed posterity the record of this case, even if it didn't turn out the way he hoped. He said, and these are his exact words, "I don't owe posterity a damn thing. If there's one thing I learned from this Revisionist business, it's that you can alter reality. I simply have a means, expedient and permanent, to ensure it: burn it all!"

He then lit the match he was holding and dropped it onto the pile of papers. With a tremendous whoosh, the mound burst into flames. We both stepped back as the flames suddenly lit up the backyard which had, only a moment before, been pitch black. As we stood watching the papers burn, Zach muttered to himself wildly, "Die, you cursed rubbish! At least I've outlived you if nothing else."

In the midst of the circle of raging flames from the barbeque, your father's face was illuminated, evincing an uncanny sort of contortion, between extreme sadness and extreme relief. Feeling I had no words to offer him in the face of those flames, I remained silent beside him, watching the pile of documents curl and burn, until your father said:

"Do you know what that smell is, Isaac?"

"Lighter fluid burning papers—what else?"

"It's the smell of history being revised. It's a wondrous smell. Inhale, take a whiff and never forget it!"

Given the intense oddity of that night and your father's bizarre behavior on that occasion, I came to believe that in order to honor your father's memory, and also not to upset family members unnecessarily, discretion would be the best course of action. Prior to this letter, I have never told anyone (including your sister and my wife, Sara) about that night. Indeed, I've never uttered a word about it, much less recounted that experience in writing, as I've done for you just now.

I do hope you will accept my sincere apology for not coming right out in our earlier correspondence and telling you of this episode and specifically how the Revisionist material came to be destroyed. In truth, as I've already said, a part of me thought it best that I keep this sad episode from the end of your father's life to myself, and I also wasn't sure what sort of impact it would have on both you and Cygnus, knowing how badly this Revisionist case affected your father.

Yet, despite the absence of the material you requested that was long ago reduced to ashes, I do hope you will still consider the possibility of my meeting with you and Cygnus.

In closing, I just wanted to add that, per your post scriptum in your last letter indicating that you have been writing both poetry and prose, I am glad to hear of it and would welcome the opportunity to read your work. Also along these lines, it might interest you to know that your sister, Sara, also has been writing, as well as drawing. Enclosed for you is a copy of one of Sara's children's books so that you can look at her literary efforts, along with her illustrations. This is a short book about the adventures of a cute dog named Prouty Spaniel that Sara wrote and illustrated, aimed at five- to eight-year-olds. The enclosed roughs are from *Prouty Spaniel Takes a Walk.*

Yours truly,
Isaac

13.
Prouty Spaniel Takes a Walk

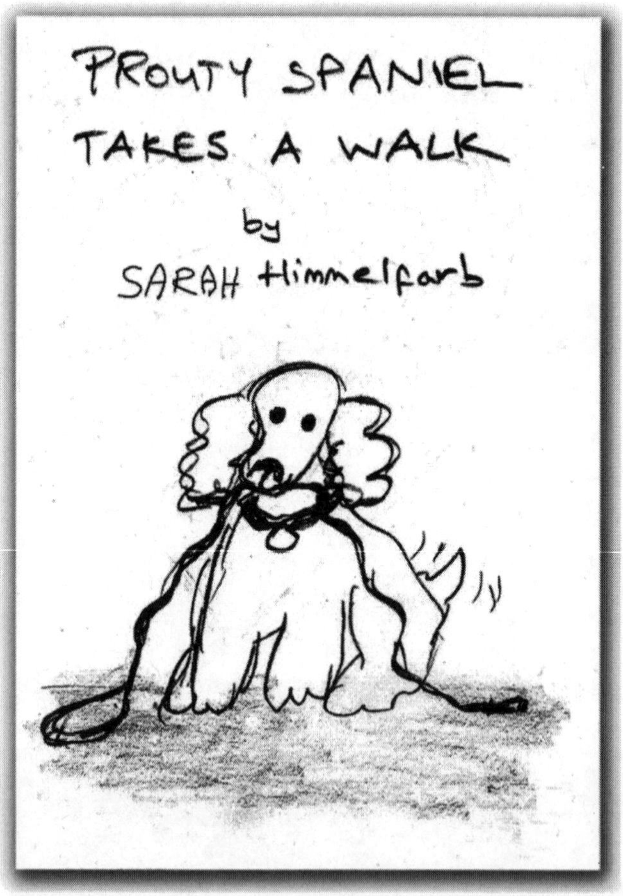

Sarah has a little dog.

She calls him Prouty.

Sarah laughs when

Prouty wags his tail.

She smiles when
Prouty smiles

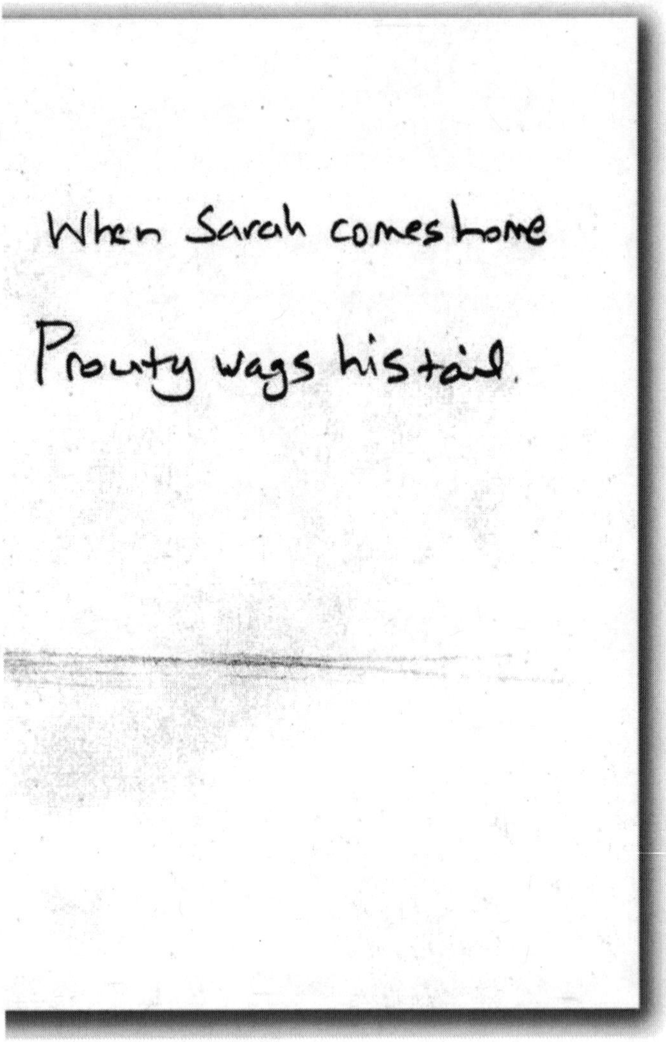

When Sarah comes home

Prouty wags his tail.

Sarah gives Prouty
his food.

SPROUTY

Sarah gives Prouty
his water.

PROUTY

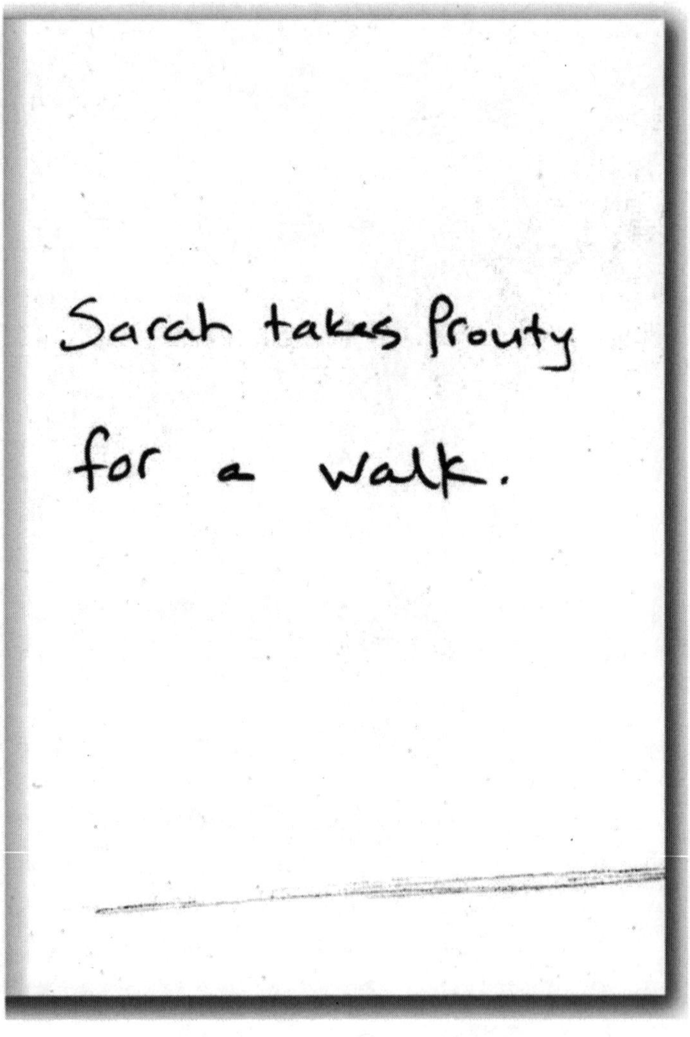

Sarah takes Prouty

for a walk.

Prouty frowns

at the rain.

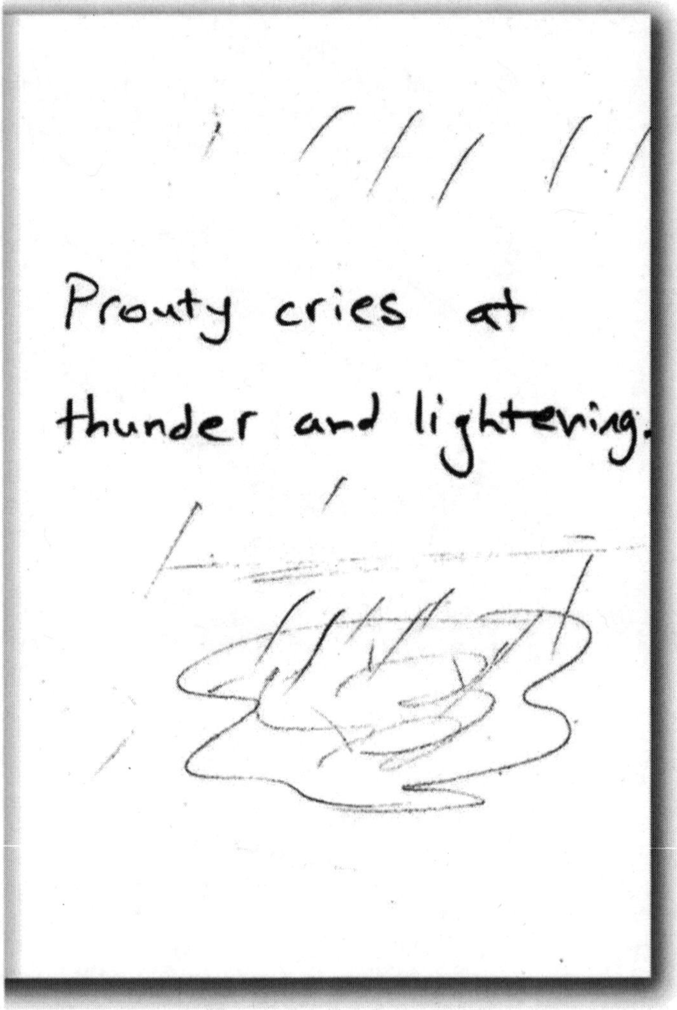
Prouty cries at
thunder and lightening.

When Sarah is there,
Prouty does not cry
when there is
thunder and
lightening.

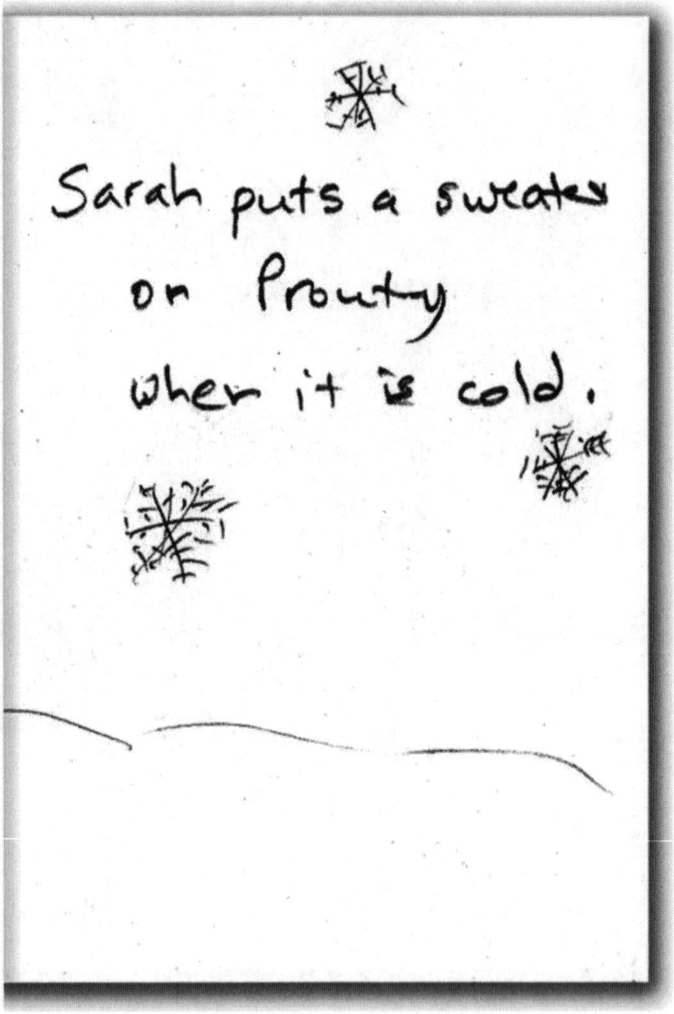
Sarah puts a sweater
on Prouty
when it is cold.

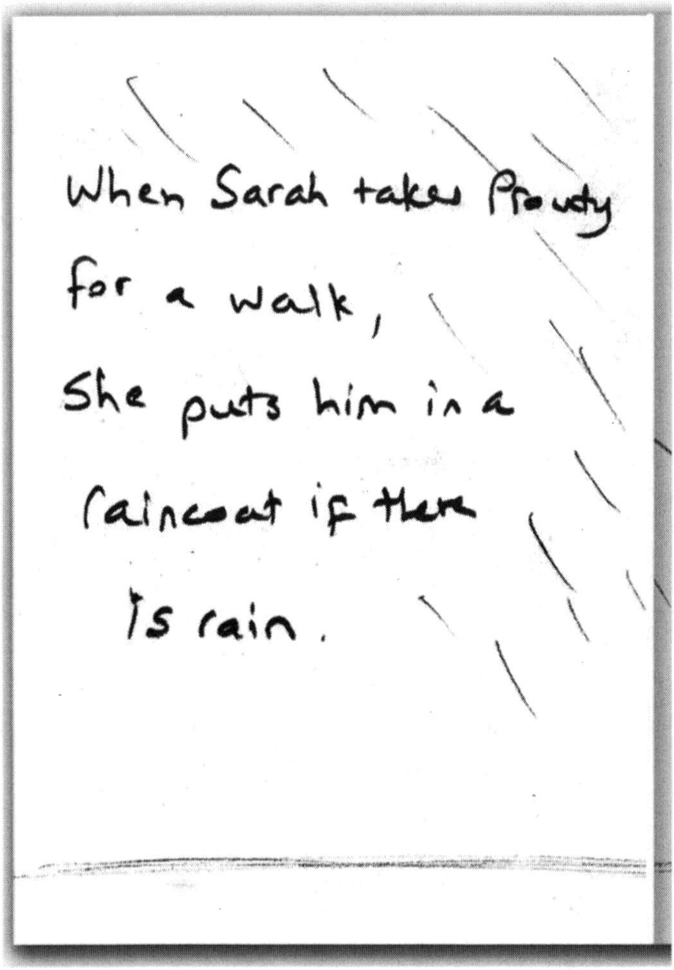
When Sarah takes Prouty
for a walk,
She puts him in a
raincoat if there
is rain.

Sarah runs with
Prouty and plays
outside.
She throws sticks
for Prouty to pick up.

She throws a big ball
to Prouty.

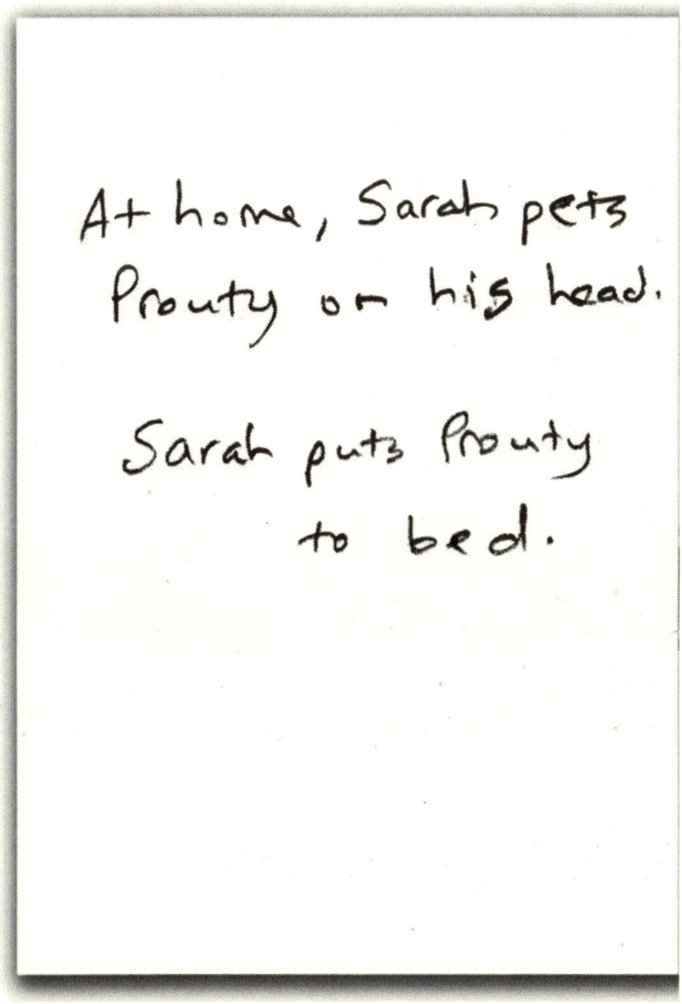

At home, Sarah pets
Prouty on his head.

Sarah puts Prouty
to bed.

14.
Notes from *The Revisionist: A Case of Logokinesis Mania*

Dr. Zachary Weiss

After J demonstrated his logokinetic ability with the texts relating to Jung and by Wordsworth, I wanted to challenge him with longer, more complex works like novels. I presented J with a copy of Stephen King's *The Shining*. J, being very familiar with this work, quickly scanned the text, then asked if it would bother me much if he logokinetically eliminated from the book multiple passages he found extraneous, including all references to marauding shrubbery. I replied that not only would it not bother me at all, but I would be fascinated to observe him revising the text exactly as he proposed, if he felt both comfortable and confident that he could do so in my office at that time. J thanked me for the opportunity to Logokinetically "correct" the text, as he put it, and then noted those passages that had always struck him as some of the weakest writing in a book that otherwise he regarded to be perhaps Stephen King's best.

I was excited to see further confirmation of J's abilities, and so sat silently as he perused the text, then closed his eyes, then after many minutes of silence between us, he passed the book across my desk back to me, looking a bit fatigued as he did so. J was staring at the floor and seemed a bit short of breath as I quickly scanned King's book, noting that the contrast I recalled between the sinister quality of the hotel and the topiary outside of the hotel—all of the language dwelling on the shrubs—had been eliminated. Then, before I could hazard a remark, as our time was up and J looked physically exhausted, he apologized about not being able to discuss what he'd just done, since he needed to go home and take a nap.

As J's was my last session of the day, I decided to leave the office early, a few minutes after he had departed, and took his altered version of *The Shining* with me. As I was driving home, an irresistible thought struck me. Between my office and home, I knew I would be passing a Barnes & Noble bookstore. As I approached the bookstore, by sheer chance I saw an empty parking space just in front of the store, and so I pulled over, parked, fed the meter, and went into the store with my briefcase containing J's modified version of King's text.

In no time at all, I located *The Shining* on a shelf, quickly pulled it down and opened it at the last page. The volume in the store was 403 pages long. I then took J's version from my briefcase and found that his was 381 pages. After confirming both volumes were from the same publisher and same edition, I had to accept that the very length of the book was shorter than before J had mentally eliminated what he felt to be extraneous and unnecessary material.

However, the next day, I noticed that, just like the initial incident with the text of my Freud book, his modification of Karl Jung's biography and Wordsworth's poem, the Stephen King novel had reverted to both its original text and its original length of 403 pages.

Still we pressed on: In our next session, I gave him Hemingway's *The Old Man and The Sea* and found that he reduced the length of the book by one-third by removing most of Hemingway's interminable addresses by the old man to the fish, which didn't really move the story along and were embarrassingly maudlin, using, as J explained, Hemingway's much superior early story from the 1930's, *The Undefeated*, as a model. In the end, J produced what I had to admit was a much stronger story than the famous one currently in print.

Again, however, the text and size of the book returned to its original dimensions within a day.

Still, J amused me in small ways, changing the famous opening of Dante's *Inferno*, which read: "When the path was no longer straight," to "When the path had turned quite gay." Admittedly, this side of his work was no doubt a bit childish, but it provided further proof that J did have his remarkable Logokinetic ability, and I was pleased to see in this edit some indication as to his state of mind progressing positively such that he could allow himself human/ silly moments.

15.
Letter from Magnus Pater, né Abram Weiss

The Society of the Divine Receptor
Wild Brush Ranch
Modesto, CA 90634
Phone: (914) 634-6660
Fax: (914) 634-6661
Website: wwwIAMIT.com

His Serene Receptor,
Seven Times Blessed
By the Kisses of Moses,
The Embraces of Jesus
And the Caresses of Buddha,
Solidified by the Spectral Handler
Magnus Pater Sends Greetings
To You, Dr. Isaac Himmelfarb,
on this day, July 22, 2018

We thank you for our former sister's work. It is blessed that she loves animals so. It is our recollection from our former childhood that it was Sara and not some companion animal that was frightened of thunder and lightning, but it is fine if she now attributes that sensitivity to a puppy. Animals possess the understanding that thunder and lightning are divine punctuations from the Spectral Handler.

It is with sorrow, however, that we hear of Sara's distress.

The Spectral Handler has advised us that a trouble Sara has been afflicted with is a personal loss that lured her to the cloud of alcohol. It was a loss that tore something that had become a part of her and left her bereft, as if something that had been growing in her was taken from her.

We have been advised by our spiritual counselors that though it is not entirely clear what was growing in our former sister and no longer is, Sara needs help. We do want to help dear Sara at our abode. We have aided many lost souls like our former sister. Therefore, we think it wise that you and she should come here to aid her in the healing of her loss. Additionally, the Spectral Handler has suggested it would bring us great pleasure to visit with both our former sister, Sara, as well as our former childhood playmate—you, Isaac.

Concerning healing, our guides have whispered to us that the course of action our former father took in destroying the material related to the case of the Revisionist was not a cure. Indeed, his passing from cancer was accelerated by such an act, for in destroying the revisionist papers, our former father destroyed a major part of himself. But, despite such an act, as Saint Paul wrote in his Epistle to the Corinthians, "Nothing is hidden that shall not be revealed."

The energy behind the words of those documents he burned in our former backyard is still out there. Paper may burn but the words written thereon can never be destroyed, for their thoughts are eternal. Indeed, our guides spoke of a way as yet unstated to recover our former father's words through the agency of Cygnus.

Indeed, as Cygnus told us, we know our former father tried persuading others at Colombia University that Cygnus had a remarkable talent to alter the printed word by willpower, which did not require healing but recognition. Cygnus told us how the examination at Colombia was a total failure and my former father suffered such humiliation that he was forced to retire from his profession.

We are not sure if you are aware, Isaac, but Cygnus, writing under his former name, William Pierce, was able to obtain a copy of the transcript of that examination through a letter to the University explaining his right, as the test subject, to all records pertaining to this examination.

Cygnus's departure from my former father's care ultimately led this young man to our domicile. With at least a copy of this transcript in our possession, according to Lord Jesus, Buddha, Moses and the Spectral Handler, we now accept that the time is propitious for you to see the young man you seem so curious to meet and for us to have the opportunity to reunite with our former sister, Sara, and offer her the succor we know she can find at our abode.

Post Scriptum: For the kind gift of our former sister's Book and her accompanying illustrations, we shall send, as we indicated earlier, two poems from our collection of Poetry, *The Song of the Purpled Realm*, since according to your report, our former father's documents are no longer available for our perusal.

ARTICULATED BY THE GRACE OF THE SPECTRAL HANDLER,
Magnus Pater

16.
Transcript of the Examination of J

TRANSCRIPT OF THE EXAMINATION
OF J, A PSYCHIATRIC PATIENT,
TO EVALUATE HIS CLAIM
OF HIS CAPACITY
TO ALTER MATTER
THROUGH MENTAL ABILITY

March 15, 2007

Department of Psychology
Franklin Hall, Room 322
Columbia University

ABSTRACT

This document is attested to be a fair and accurate transcript by the board of examiners conducting the examination held on March 15, 2007 at 10 A.M. to ascertain whether the patient of Dr. Zachary Weiss (referred to hereinafter as J) could verify his claim to be able to alter printed texts through the exercise of a unique mental ability named by Dr. Weiss as Logokinetic Mania.

The board of examiners comprised Dr. Alberto DePasquale, Dr. Simone Denker and Dr. Phillip Brennan, whose areas of specialty are respectively abnormal psychology and neurological disorders. Operating the camcorder mounted on a tripod to record the examination was a student from the Drama Department, Ms. Amber Mink. The moderator was Dr. Denker. All three examiners had received a preliminary report from Dr. Weiss explaining the nature and character of J's alleged ability to be demonstrated on this occasion.

TRANSCRIPT

Dr. Simone Denker: Good morning everyone. For the record, I am Dr. Simone Denker, the moderator for today's examination. On my left is Dr. Alberto DePasquale, while on my right is Dr. Phillip Brennan. We all have read your preliminary report, Dr. Weiss, which outlines J's alleged ability to alter physically printed text through mental ability. Doctor Weiss, are you ready to proceed?

Dr. Zachary Weiss: Yes, I am.

Dr. Denker: J, are you ready?

J: What?

Dr. Denker: J, would you please stop looking at Ms. Mink and focus on the matter at hand?

J: Oh, yes, I'm sorry.

Ms. Mink: Sorry.

Dr. Denker: Alright, may we get started here? J, do you feel comfortable with this sort of test?

J: I am, though I want to warn you that my talent may be best demonstrable with people whom I know and feel I can trust. Also, sometimes, I can't control my edits and whatever pops into my head might show up on the page. I don't want anybody to think that I or Doctor Weiss are lying to you if this doesn't work. I also don't want you to think I'm crazy.

Dr. Denker: Don't worry. You are safe here, J. We all only want what is best for you. In any event, if you are comfortable with it, J, having read Dr. Weiss's report, my colleagues and I have designed a twofold test to determine whether Dr. Weiss's claims can be verified. You, J, need not worry if these tests succeed or fail; this is all merely an inquiry, about which none of us wants you to feel any discomfort or pressure. There is no wrong or right outcome. Whatever happens is fine; we all just want you to feel at your ease and we all appreciate you being here and participating today. I do hope you understand that.

J: I understand; I'm fine.

Dr Denker: Great, then let's get started. Set out on the table in front of you are three randomly chosen books, Herman Melville's *Moby Dick*, Henry James's *What Maisie Knew and Other Stories*, and Vladimir Nabokov's *Laughter in the Dark*. Ms. Mink is, as of now, running the camcorder which is focused on the books on the table. This will provide recorded visual verification for whatever results, or lack thereof, that this test will provide. So, J, we ask you now, if you do not mind, to go to the room next door, peruse the three books and then tell us when you are finished with your revisions. During this time, as you read and make your changes to the texts, Ms. Mink will record all that transpires. After that point, Dr. Weiss will go to another room to see if you, J, have changed the texts in question. Afterward, we will all inspect the results both in the texts, as well as the videotaped evidence in the separate rooms provided by Ms. Mink. We shall also examine the tapes from the camcorder to see if any of your changes correspond with those perceived by Dr. Weiss. Finally, we'll look at the printed texts themselves to see for ourselves if any changes in the language on any pages are apparent.

(Hiatus in discussion: timed 25 minutes, from 10:12 A.M. to 10:37 A.M. Everyone then assembles again in the lecture hall after break, viewing videotape that shows first J at a desk alone in a room, then Dr. Weiss in another room.)

J: (On videotape #1) I'm finished. What I've done is insert new opening sentences for each book. These are admittedly odd edits. Instead of "Call me Ishmael," the text for *Moby Dick* now reads, "Call me Horny." For the Nabokov novel, I've inserted an entirely new sentence as the first line in the book: "No one's getting laid." As for *What Maisie Knew*, the copy I have now begins with "Maisie knew how to dress for sin."

Miss Mink: (*Giggling audibly*) I'm so sorry. Please forgive me.

J: (*Looking up from books and smiling at Miss Mink*) No problem. I'm glad you enjoyed my edits.

(End of videotape #1)

Dr. Weiss: (on videotape #2): Ms. Mink, I cannot help but wonder that you may have had an influence on J's edits. I see that J changed the opening to Melville's masterpiece from "Call me Ishmael" to "Call me Horny." Also, I have to say J's opening to the Nabakov novel is rather crude: "No one's getting laid". Worst of all, the new sentence he added as the first line in *What Maisie Knew*, "Maisie knew how to dress for sin," is rather perverse since Maisie was just a child in the story. Okay, I've seen all I need to. If you don't mind, Miss Mink, you can tell the board they can now examine the books themselves to see J's and our results confirmed.

(End of videotape #2)

Miss Mink: (*Giggling audibly while screening the videotapes*) I'm sorry Doctors.

Dr. Weiss: Please, let's all recall the reason we are here today is quite serious.

J: I'm sorry, but I did warn everyone, sometimes I can't control my edits.

Dr. Denker: Don't worry at all J. As I said earlier, there is no right or wrong here and we do appreciate you participating, but at this point, could you please step out of the room while we discuss the test results?

(J gets up and leaves the room, after which the videotapes are screened three more times)

Dr. Denker: Dr. Weiss, are you absolutely sure about this?

Dr. Weiss: Yes, of course. You saw the videotape; you saw how J and I independently of each other confirmed the changes rendered to the texts.

Dr. Denker: Unfortunately, looking through these books, I don't see any of these changes that J claimed to have made and you, somehow—I'm not entirely clear how—confirmed.

Dr. DePasquale: I too must concur with my colleague, Dr. Denker, I do not see any of these changes either, and I am entirely baffled as to how the two of you came up with the same changes to the texts.

Dr. Brennan: Bottom line, Dr. Weiss: it matters little to me that you and your patient somehow repeated edits that no one else can see. This was not scheduled to be some magic show in a tent where the public comes to see tricks performed; rather, we are all professionals in a highly regarded academic institution. We assembled today to see whether, as you alleged, your patient could change printed language on a page, and after indulging this fantastic claim, we are all left facing books that show absolutely no change whatsoever to the words printed in them.

Dr. Weiss: I don't understand. I swear to all of you that I saw the changes in the texts in question when I was in that room. Of course, from the first videotape, it appears, by the way J is scrunching up his eyebrows and looking flirtatiously at Miss Mink, that he was not focused on the task at hand. However, I know what I saw. Even if the books in front of you now, apparently show no changes, and so seem to contradict my claim, again, I know what I saw. I must tell you now, on multiple occasions in the past, I have seen J alter a text, and then that text reverted back to the original the next day. However, I have never seen his Logokinetic edits revert back as rapidly as they apparently did today. I, myself, am baffled.

Dr. Denker: Dr. Weiss, I'll admit that none of us can explain how you and J read the exact same sentences from the texts that J claimed to alter. Still, from what we've seen, we're very concerned about your level of your attachment to your patient. It appears you've gotten so close to him that you've compromised your objectivity in his case.

Dr. Brennan: My observations of the patient (superficial as they may be, since this is the first time I've ever seen him), suggest to me that (with his excited, emphatic way of speaking) he is suffering from nothing more exotic than delusions deriving from manic depression.

Dr. DePasquale: Yes, yes, I concur. I've had patients who, when in the manic phase of manic depression, claimed they could alter the color of the wall paper in their room through sheer willpower alone. I am surprised, Dr. Weiss, that you didn't consider this.

Dr. Weiss: Of course, I did. That was, in fact, my preliminary diagnosis.

Dr. DePasquale: Is it possible, Dr. Weiss, you might be a victim of *folie à deux*?

Dr. Brennan: Dr. Weiss, it may be a strong possibility. Perhaps, in some way that science cannot yet explain, you have somehow connected so closely to your patient that you actually were able to pick up how J would have altered those texts, and thus were able to repeat exactly what he claimed to have done. While that in itself is quite curious, it is not at all remotely demonstrative of your so-called Logokinetic mania, which was the reason we assembled here today, but instead may be demonstrative of your losing control of the normally proscribed boundaries practiced by all competent psychoanalysts between the analyst and the analysand.

Dr. Weiss: Dr. Brennan, your remarks strike me as entirely insulting and as too rapidly reaching for a convenient conclusion that denigrates the integrity of my work over the course of a long and respected career.

Dr. Brennan: Let's be clear, I've no wish to diminish the contributions you've made in our field, Dr. Weiss, rather, I am just offering as a possibility the thought that J is such a persuasive individual that he can persuade others, even accomplished analysts like you, into sharing his delusion?

Dr. Denker: Dr. Weiss, you do have to admit that is a possibility.

Dr. Weiss: I don't have to admit any such thing. J has real ability; I have seen it.

Dr. Denker: Unfortunately though, Dr. Weiss, it has not been demonstrated here. Perhaps one way in which we might reconcile the apparent failure of this examination to prove the existence of your patient's so-called Logokinetic mania is at least to entertain the notion that J can target people he knows and trusts to share in his delusion. Why not call it "targeted *folie à deux*?"

Dr. DePasquale: Dr. Denker, that's actually quite fascinating, but, the facts are the facts: nothing today could be verified by objective scientific standards. The printed texts have not changed, therefore, nothing that we came here today to evaluate has been objectively verified.

Dr. Weiss: But none of you understand: This test was flawed! Ms. Mink was wearing a provocative dress, which might be appropriate for the Drama Department and whatever play they are putting on, but not for this examination. That said, I suggest this test was compromised by Ms. Mink and her sexually provocative dress. As psychoanalytic professionals, we all know how intensely, in various patients, sexual stimuli can impact on a patient's behavior and even fundamental abilities.

Dr. DePasquale: That, Dr. Weiss, is an argument which cannot be verified—while your idea about Ms. Mink's influence on this test is unusual, it is also impossible to prove.

Dr. Weiss: You don't understand. None of you are even trying to understand. You're all responding in such a reductive manner to J's unique talent.

Dr. Brennan: Dr. Weiss, I insist, in the best interest of your own mental health—which this test actually may have brought into question—and in the best interest of your patient moving forward toward overcoming his psychosis, that you to refer your patient to another therapist, who will not encourage J's illness, as you seem to, but rather will work toward its cure. Additionally, I urge you, Dr. Weiss, to take a leave of absence from your practice for health reasons and undergo an intensive regimen of psychoanalysis yourself.

Dr. Weiss: I protest. You're all wrong. J is talented. You've just failed to come up with the right kind of test to demonstrate Logokinesis Mania! And as for you, Brennan, just who the hell do you think you are to be judging me? Listen Brennan, you were picking your nose back in pre-med classes when I'd already launched my own practice and was well into my career. You're nothing more than an insolent puppy chasing your own tail while pretending to evaluate the serious potential psychoanalytic advances true professionals are exploring!

Dr. Denker: I'm so sorry Dr. Weiss that the outcome of

today's experiment wasn't what you had hoped for. However, as we are all professionals here, certainly we need not resort to insults or personal attacks. Additionally, I'd like to remind you, Dr. Brennan, that our focus today is on the patient J, not Dr. Weiss. Still, Dr. Weiss, both you and your patient agreed to the format of today's experiment. Now that is complete, by the terms of this format, your patient was unable to demonstrate the ability you claimed him to be capable of. Of course, it is worthy of note, that it was extremely unusual that both you and J recited the same alleged alterations to the language of the texts we selected. Yet, as the Board of Examiners found no physical proof demonstrating that the texts were changed in print, the Board has been left with no concrete physical proof to demonstrate that your patient J's alleged ability actually exists.

Dr. Weiss: Listen, I know what I saw and what I believe. I spent several years studying J's Logokinetic abilities before I brought them to you. I never would have undertaken to bother the Board if I had not actually encountered concrete evidence myself from J that led me fully to believe that in the course of his treatment I had uncovered a new and, as yet, untapped potential of humanity's psychological capacity.

Dr. Depasquale: Dr. Weiss, I'm sorry, but this examination is over.

Dr. Denker: I'm afraid I must concur. In one week, Dr. Weiss, you will receive our formal conclusions. As for now, this meeting is officially adjourned.

CONCLUSION REACHED ON THE RESULTS OF THE EXPERIMENT

In the view of the board of examiners, comprised of Dr. Simone Denker, Dr. Phillip Brennan and Dr. Alberto DePasquale, Dr. Zachary Weiss's patient, J, was unable to demonstrate or in any way even partially substantiate his claims to be able physically to alter printed text through the exercise of a previously unknown mental ability. The board recommends that Dr. Weiss refer his patient to another analyst. If he fails to do so, we will recommend that disciplinary action be taken against Dr. Weiss by the Professional Standards and Conduct Board of the American Psychiatric Association.

So attested March 20, 2007:

Dr. Simone Denker
Dr. Phillip Brennan
Dr. Alberto DePasquale

17.
Excerpt from *The Revisionist: A Case of Logokinesis Mania*

Dr. Zachary Weiss

Looking back on J's case now that, per the committee's directive, I no longer treat J—although I still loathe that asshole Brennan, I even vividly recall how he seemed to be smirking at me as we all left at the end of the meeting and how I wanted to wipe that idiotic expression off his fucking face with my fist—I am convinced now more than ever that J's condition hardly warrants dismissal, as these idiotic so-called experts concluded, but rather J's condition can be seen everywhere and entirely warrants further intense scrutiny.

After all, if one looks at the horrible history of much of the twentieth century, maybe J's condition was shared in different ways among many of the past century's worst political monsters: Hitler, Stalin, Mao, Pol Pot, and others. They all seemed to have the same manipulative power to make people believe in the most fantastic nonsense, deriving from their ideal edits and revisions of history, with the most horrendous results when trying to actualize their fantasies.

Just open your goddamn eyes and it's obvious that J's Logokinetic mania was fundamentally (in one way or another) also at the core of all of the most maniacal leaders, dictators and regimes. Look at the history of the Soviet Union. Under Stalin, it was common to airbrush out of official Kremlin photographs people who had fallen out of favor. Such a practice produced bizarre, surreal results, such as photographs showing only the right arm of a person who had previously been in Stalin's favor, but had then somehow fallen under suspicion and been eliminated; his image removed from the picture, leaving only the glimpse of his remaining arm. Of course Stalin knew the power of Revisionism.

Milan Kundera, the Czech writer, noted this phenomenon in his own country during the Communist period, in his novel *The Unbearable Lightness of Being*, where a photo thus retouched is described. The only thing that remained of the deleted individual was his hat, so that it appeared to be floating in mid-air amid a group of Czech Communist officials.

This photographic evidence of editing or revising history, bearing such a clear resemblance to J's Logokinetic mania, is hardly unique or exclusive to J's case or present history. The desire to revise invades every aspect of culture, from high to low. As J reminded me in one of our last sessions, when he refused to sit, instead pacing up and down my office, sweating profusely, "There's that song, 'I'm Gonna Wash That Man Right Out of My Hair', from that famous Broadway musical, *South Pacific*." At this point he stopped pacing and stared at me, "C'mon, how can you deny it? It's human nature that we want to revise our lives, eliminate from our memory the people who made us unhappy."

Noting his agitated state in that session, I remained silent and still, as J asserted that the government did tinker with our individual memories of each citizen's past, revising our memories of Vietnam or President Kennedy's assassination. Despite all he said, as I sat there silently watching him pace and sweat, I realized J wouldn't budge from his conviction that such revisionism—so much more broadly applied than merely on the page, as he did—was possible.

J then mentioned how he had found that poets from Robert Browning to W. H. Auden and Robert Lowell, even Jacob Miller, endlessly revised their work long after they were first published. "So," he asked me, "who is to say what is the true version of any work when all work is endlessly subject to revision?"

But I must confess, even before scheduling the experiment before the Board of Examiners at Columbia, in our sessions I was guilty of pushing J more and more to keep demonstrating his Logokinesis Mania. With each different text in which I saw his mental edits appear, I was becoming more obsessed with the prospects of showing J's extraordinary and entirely unique ability to others, knowing and already anticipating how my discovery would add a luster to my reputation that no other psychiatrist in living memory would be able match. So, of course, I couldn't resist the opportunity to demonstrate my discovery before the Board of Examiners—it was just a matter of time—hell, to be perfectly honest, for months before the day of the experiment, I had wrestled with insomnia, tossing and turning at night imagining the various possible wordings I could use so that it might most readily make its way into the next edition of the DSM, which would be validated by my work with J and the positive findings of the Board of Examiners.

But on the actual day of the examination, how was I to anticipate that some slender, but buxom, silly young woman, Ms. Mink, would show up in a tight-fitting, imitation black Chanel dress, sucking on a lollipop? She probably had come from a rehearsal of some play and didn't have time to change out of her costume, which was wildly inappropriate for J's examination. She was on loan, I later learned, from the Drama Department, but this did little to alleviate my concerns that J might not be able to control his Logokinetic mania when sexual factors intervened. This had not been a concern when J had his sessions in my office where there was nothing of a sexual nature to distract him from demonstrating his abilities in the quasi-antiseptic environment of only us two men sitting on opposite sides of my desk and, as J was heterosexual, any issues related to his sexuality had never arisen in our sessions.

However, with the gifts of 20/20 hindsight, looking back on the case of J today, I can see now that quite likely I was so singularly focused on J's rare Logokinetic ability in our work together that I did not adequately explore any issues related to J's own sexuality, as I always routinely did with all my other patients.

Thus, on the day of the examination at Columbia, when I saw J thoroughly distracted by Ms. Mink, I realized, albeit too late, that I had negligently omitted from J's psychiatric equation the factor of his all-too-human sexuality. Of course, a young man with hormones raging, having been brought face-to-face with an attractive young woman, J, in his sexually stimulated and distracted state, could offer only temporary revisions, which looked coarse and absurd, given his far greater focus on the attractive Ms. Mink than any page of print we might have put before him.

Although in all my experiments with J's Logokinetic mania in my office, his editorial changes were always of limited duration, they usually lasted at least several hours, not minutes, as seems to have been the case in the test at Columbia. That his edits lasted just long enough for me to read them from each text, but his edits did *not* last long enough for the Board of Examiners to see them, only made me look foolish to everybody.

Even before anyone on the Board uttered a word, a few minutes passed in horrific silence as I observed each of the members looking back and forth between the texts and me and then at each other. Oddly, when the Board looked at me in those agonizing silent minutes, it seemed they were staring at me as if I had become the patient under scrutiny, not J—indeed, I had the very concrete and definite feeling that I was now being looked at as the subject of the experiment, and not J. Yes, my feelings went beyond a sense that I was being regarded as foolish to something even worse. Again, I could not help but observe, as they were observing me, how they seemed to be struggling to maintain the professional poker face that is de rigueur in the field of psychiatry, yet I also noted how a few broke their poker faces to suggest what I thought might be a glimpse of compassion—or was it pity?—It all was unclear and left me wanting to break the silence by shouting at the Board: "Well, what the hell's the matter, goddamnit?"

I had sensed incredulity from the examiners almost from the start. Dr. Denker said the right things to J to put him at ease, but I sensed she wasn't truly giving us a chance and, in fact, wanted to be elsewhere, and my suspicions were confirmed when Dr.

Denker, in her impatience, began discreetly yet repeatedly looking at her watch while she was asking her questions in the Q and A portion of the examination. Dr. Brennan, on the other hand, was much worse; after perusing the texts, he appeared on the brink of becoming openly hostile to me, as if our examination had been entirely a waste of his invaluable time and an insult to his professional integrity. As all of this was transpiring, inasmuch as I had read J's crude and borderline vulgar edits as they appeared on the page before me, I was entirely baffled by the behavior of the Board of Examiners who had not, at that point, made it clear to me that, to them, J's Logokinetically edited texts were in no way shown on any of the pages in front of them. Only later, when I was made aware that such was the case, was I able to understand what initially had struck me as the rude if not outright bizarre behavior of the Board.

But to hell with those hacks; what's left to consider? I can no longer work with J, but even if I could, why cultivate a skill that reduces everything to ephemera and has not been confirmed by others? J's talent has already made it impossible for me to see fixity in anything. But say I can accept the notion that what we see might be temporal, if I'm alone in that perception, as it seems that I now am among my colleagues, this leaves my role as a psychiatrist in the eyes of my peers entirely obsolete. So why do I still even bother to scribble away at this monograph?

18.
The Diary of Isaac Himmelfarb

7/27/18

Well, it appears that Abram/Magnus bought my story about the burning of Zach's documents, which is precisely what I'd wanted and needed to advance my learning more about the case of J, yet I feel a tad guilty that my letter with its lies yielded such easy, promising results. Of course, I'm both excited at the prospect of meeting Cygnus, J, or whatever he likes to call himself, as well as the prospect of helping to bring about a family reunion between a brother and a sister so long separated from each other—though I do have some lingering fears that my wife's seeing her brother in such an unstable condition might have a deleterious impact on her own delicate state. Still, I am hoping in the long run that bringing Sara and Abram together might be a truly positive thing for both of them, not to mention that meeting the patient who demolished my mentor's career might offer a unique opportunity for me as a psychanalyst.

Looking back at Abram's last letter, though, I have to confess it was a bit eerie that I palpably felt Abram somehow guessed Sara had a miscarriage and that was what had tipped her into alcoholism. Abram was always extraordinarily sensitive to other people's state of mind, even if it appeared he was lost in a fog of his very own and located hundreds of miles away on the other end of the country.

Bottom line, though, my letter was successful in generating an invite from Abram to visit his commune, as well as getting his promise to send a sample of his recent literary efforts. If these works are anything like his letters, they should prove to be interesting to say the least.

Additionally, Abram's letter revealed that, despite his state of mind, he was able to get hold of the transcript of Zach's disastrous test in front of his colleagues at Colombia, which failed to demonstrate the supposed abilities of J. As I've noted, it seems Abram is resourceful even if demented. Magnus seems to have inveigled Cygnus to ask for the transcript of the examination from Colombia so that he could examine it. The test was a matter of public record, and since J was one of the central parties to the examination, I suspect that legally Colombia was obligated to provide the transcript to him.

It's interesting, though, that J only asked for the transcript while at Magnus's compound. Professionally, of course, it would have been irresponsible for Zach to have offered J a copy of the transcript. Zach wouldn't have wanted J exposed to such a psychologically devastating blow as reading a document which labeled him a poor, deluded individual. Zach, even with his own upset over the Colombia results, I have to hope, would still have retained enough professional integrity to have wanted to protect the interests of his former patient as much as possible, even if he could no longer treat him, as per the Colombia Board's order he assign J to another therapist.

No doubt after the examination, Zach would have been too upset, too distracted to think that J might have cared to see a copy of the transcript. However, after reading an entry in Zach's monograph, which he wrote shortly after the failed Columbia experiment, it now strikes me that Zach must have felt no small amount of guilt at having built up J's hopes about his ability to demonstrate the reality of Logokenisis mania, which Zach, in the end, must have realized he was doing, not to help his patient so much as to advance his own career—to leave his mark.

It's curious, if I separate myself from my happy childhood memories with Abram, despite the fact that Abram now seems so far to be the most psychotic of any person I've ever actually encountered, he somehow seems to have retained a practical side to himself. Indeed, oddly, I can only assume it was Abram, Zach's son, who had his acolyte, Cygnus, confront the business end of securing a copy of the Colombia transcript, which Zach, the professional psychiatrist, was unable to do. Perhaps, in the end, it's up to the next generation sometimes to handle certain complex matters which overwhelm earlier generations and remain lingering for the future on the border of uncertainty.

In any event, I think the timing is great in that it offers Sara the opportunity to see her long-lost brother and both of us to get to meet the mysterious J, who had such an enormous impact on Sara and Abram's father's life. Abram's offer to open the door leaves me, I believe, with no choice but to walk through it. Indeed, our meeting all together—Abram, Sara, J and myself—is truly the best thing I could have hoped for from my correspondence with Abram.

Should I have told Sara from the get-go, as soon as I came across the Spireman report, that I'd a lead on Abram's whereabouts, and then, indeed, one might easily ask why didn't I tell her once I'd got in touch with her long-lost brother? What can I say? The longer this went on, the more I was sucked into the mystery and could only see a happy ending, with Sara thrilled when I finally reunited her with her brother.

19.
Letter to Magnus Pater, né Abram Weiss

Isaac A. Himmelfarb, M.D.
Clinical Psychiatrist,
Specialist in Child Psychology
4 East 89th Street
New York, NY 10028
Phone: (212) 347-5678
E-mail: Ishim@msn.com

July 27, 2018

Dear Magnus,

Your insights into Sara's recent troubles are truly remarkable. Yes, Sara not only lost her father, but shortly before that she suffered a miscarriage in which she lost our child. As you so accurately seem to have assessed, albeit not explicitly, yet with some sort of amazing intuition, the almost simultaneous double loss of both the family patriarch and the child that would have represented the start of the next generation of the family—losing both the older generation and the future generation of family—led to Sara's increased drinking. I was thinking it would be wonderful if we could arrange a trip not only to see you for a long overdue family reunion, but also to meet Cygnus. I know Sara has missed you, her brother, so much for so many years that if both of you could reconnect, such a reunion could lighten the

kind of fucking husband are you? You think you can find out my brother is alive, even where he is, and communicate with him, and not bother to fucking tell me? Do you have the slightest goddamn clue what it means to be a husband, to know what it means to someone to know if their brother is alive or not? You've got your fancy degree and you don't know shit! And I thought I knew you—I could love you and trust you! Fuck you, Isaac!"

The next morning, Sara came out in her bathrobe and sweatpants, as if she was torn between climbing back into bed or going for a run, but she made coffee without talking to me and sat at the kitchen table chain smoking cigarettes in silence, though I'd no idea she was back to smoking. After a few cigarettes and her second cup of coffee, she began interrogating me like she was a different person, not my wife, not my sweetie Sara, but a cold, grim faced cop anxious to glean the missing facts she needed.

After I'd revealed that Abram was living in Modesto, California as the cult leader of some sort of mixed-stew New Age religion he'd concocted and, on top of everything else, that by sheer coincidence he'd ended up running into Sara's father's former patient J and taking him into his commune, Sara wanted to know if I'd revealed to Abram the work I'd been doing on their father's papers. When I admitted to Sara that I'd lied to Abram about the state of Zach's writings on the Revisionist Case, Sara simply asked, "Why?" and waited for my response.

Although I tried to explain to Sara the impact her father's writings might have on two people trapped in their own psychotic delusions, trying as best I could to simplify the complex psychanalytic perils involved in the case to language a lay person might find understandable, Sara wasn't buying my reasoning—what actually was my own version of revising reality for her brother, albeit in what I thought was in the best interests of both my wife and her brother; it was still me revising my own inner machinations no less than J revising texts at random for Zach.

"Ize, I don't know if lying to Abram was a smart move. He was always incredibly intuitive and could ultimately figure out if someone was telling him lies."

After I calmed Sara down by explaining to her my fictional

account of her father's having burned all his documents related to the Revisionist case and how I'd related these details to her brother and received a letter from him suggesting he accepted my account. "Indeed, honey," I said, "your father's papers now seem to be a non-issue. Most of all, sending Abram the roughs of your children's book happily prompted him to send us two poems from a collection of poems he's written as well as his invite for us to see him, as well as your father's former patient, J or Cygnus as he now calls himself."

After that, Sara left without speaking to me, returning only around supper time. It was then that Sara announced we should go to Modesto to see her long-lost brother. But I could tell she was still upset with me for not telling her earlier about Abram's whereabouts, as that night, once again, she insisted sleeping alone in our bedroom. But that did nothing to stop me from writing Abram that both Sara and I happily accepted his invite to his commune in Modesto.

21.
Final Excerpt from *The Revisionist: A Case of Logokinesis Mania*

Dr. Zachary Weiss

Screw the well-fed puppies who call themselves psychiatrists and think they're helping others! Fuck those whiney academic snots, with their jaws raised, pronouncing their so-called "brilliant" insights through their noses. It's now clear how they're absolutely certain they know more than others, while these intellectual puppies are busy scratching at the fleas behind their ears, whining as they drag their asses through the dirt.

My so-called colleagues—Fuck the lot of them! After twenty-three years as a practitioner of psychoanalysis, having published papers of note in all the major medical journals, having rapidly received recognition in my field, and all the while closely scrutinizing the evolution of my field and the level of true ambition of others working in my field, I hate to admit that I am quite certain that in merely a century they will look back at the current state of psychoanalysis very much as we currently regard the medieval so-called practitioners of medicine who thoroughly believed in blood-letting and the application of leeches to cure medical ailments.

What have all my years of tireless work to advance the scope and depth of psychoanalysis amounted to—even with the case of J dropping into my lap—NOTHING!!! As for these idiot-assholes who passed their verdict on my work with J. and sent my career spinning down the toilet (as if they could ever perceive the difference between brilliant work and shit), they should be taken out, lined up in front of a firing squad, made to listen to the countdown, then hear the triggers pulled—the last thing they hear—and only then might there truly be hope for those the world dismisses so callously as "mentally ill."

But what the hell, do any of my insights here matter? As if any of those horn-rimmed, tight-ass shrinks would ever read my monograph seriously or make anything remotely resembling an effort to understand what I've discerned with J.

So, you spend your life trying to advance the understanding of the shared human experience and then, way too young, have to watch it all go to hell. Such is life! No one promised us a chance to go back and do a rewrite of our own lives. Though J's skills, as unique as they are, might have offered something like a chance to do exactly that—rewrite our own lives, which so many of us have longed to do.

Now, thanks to the extraordinarily insightful conclusions of the Columbia Board of Examiners, none of this will be pursued—no rewrites, no revisions, no explorations as to the malleability of that which we call "Reality." Screw it—none of it now matters. We are all stuck with the lives we have, the cards we've been dealt.

My former colleagues—let them all die miserably and let their goddamn heads be stuck on spikes!

22.
Letter from Magnus Pater, né Abram Weiss

The Society of the Divine Receptor
Wild Brush Ranch
Modesto, CA 90634
Phone: (914) 634-6660
Fax: (914) 634-6661
Website: wwwIAMIT.com

His Serene Receptor,
Seven Times Blessed
By the Kisses of Moses,
The Embraces of Jesus
And the Caresses of Buddha,
Solidified by the Spectral Handler
Magnus Pater Sends Greetings
To You, Dr. Isaac Himmelfarb,
on this day, August 2nd, 2018

We rejoice in this glorious news that Sara, our former sister, still dear in our thoughts, and you, our former childhood friend, will be coming to visit us. Our guides, as delineated by the Spectral Handler, have indicated August 26th as most propitious for your visit—based on the specifics of your flight, a driver will be waiting for you at Modesto airport.

Cygnus told us that he was most excited to meet the daughter of our former father, who tried to help him uncover his unique abilities, but failed when confronted with cruel, dogmatic pedants at Colombia University. He wants Sara to know he bears her former father no ill will for the failure of the experiment at Colombia. He felt the committee was most unjust in forcing our former father to give up treating him. It was precisely at that time, Cygnus felt, if he had been able to continue working with our former father just a bit longer, he would have been able to demonstrate to even the dullest academic his unique power to alter printed text mentally.

As we have had the incredibly good fortune, through the will of the Spectral Handler, to witness the abilities my former father identified in Cygnus as "Logokinesis Mania," we have come to understand clearly that Cygnus has nothing remotely resembling a "mania," but rather a true gift that continually fascinates us and never fails to amaze us.

Just when we think we have identified the boundaries of Cygnus's logokinetic abilities, we see that there is more that he can do, more that he can revise. Indeed, we often have difficulty sleeping and find ourselves pacing the floorboards beside our bed just considering the potential scope for what might be revised in this limited universe of ours. However, we are torn as to utilizing the powers of Cygnus, made available to us through the benevolence of the spectral handler, which we have the choice of directing or leaving untapped.

To be entirely honest with you, Isaac, upon our deepest late-night reflections, my situation with Cygnus seems to us to resemble the choice Lord Jesus made on the cross when he let himself be killed as a mortal, despite his ability to defy a human death. It strikes us his humility and restraint might just be the model we should follow when Cygnus turns to us for direction and we wrestle with all we might dream of revising in this fragile and flawed world of ours.

But forgive us for boring you with the nonsense of our insomnia—actually, we intended just to say how truly excited we are to have you and my former sister, Sara, coming to Modesto.

As for Cygnus, he is also eager to meet you, Isaac, since our former father was your mentor and, as such, Cygnus is interested in your views once he demonstrates his ability to you.

The spectral handler has indicated to us that while you are meeting with Cygnus, there will be time for our former sister, Sara, to meet with and participate in our special women's Intensive meditation group, led by our Colomba, who is uniquely gifted at connecting with those who have wrestled with the demons of drugs and alcohol and helped them to defeat these demons via, among other things, her own unique method of spinning chakras.

So, our meeting promises to be a potent union of remarkable people. Again, we await your arrival with excitement, which several of our disciples here have suggested they can actually discern in a positive and colorful change in our aura.

ARTICULATED BY THE GRACE OF THE SPECTRAL HANDLER,
Magnus Pater

BOOK THREE

Wherein the narrative transports Sara and Isaac Himmelfarb from New York to Modesto, California, and delivers them to the commune of Sara's long-lost brother, Abram, now going by the name Magnus Pater, as the leader of his own cult and his own idiosyncratic religion, of which all of the residents of the commune are adherents, including Zach's former patient, previously known only as J, now going by the name Cygnus.

1.
The Diary of Isaac Himmelfarb

8/26/18

Two hours after take-off, looking out the window at this moment from 30,000 feet above ground at the clouds below us, I must admit my initial feeling of excitement has become one of worry. What are we going to find at Abram's commune? How will Sara react when she sees her brother, after so many years apart, hailed as Magnus Pater by his followers? And what about J? Abram's letter was reassuring that J wanted to meet Sara and that he bore Zach no ill will, but is that true? And yet, has dear Sara fully digested the potential impact of her meeting the patient who brought down her father's flourishing career, just before the onset of Zach's cancer?

So many questions, yet I'm glad that Sara was finally able to doze off and looks so peaceful now. Realistically, the combination of post-partum depression, exacerbated by the loss of our baby, the death of her dad, her inability to share her grief at her mom, who is sinking further and further into the fog of Alzheimer's, plus now trying to digest the imminent prospect of seeing her eccentric (to say the least) brother, Abram, after so many years, would be enough not only to weaken, but break even the most stable individuals alive. Despite her drinking and acting out, Sara has somehow held things together barely, as if drawing on some internal source of strength I cannot fully understand. Given such a Job-like line-up of losses for my dear Sara, I am relieved that my upping her dose of Zoloft has at least let her drift off into a blissful sleep. Albeit no doubt an illusion, she looks peaceful and, as things are, I'll happily accept the illusion.

But as a bit of turbulence now hits the plane, even as I'm writing this, I'm reminded that what looks peaceful and still on the surface often masks a raging storm beneath. I know that Sara's turbulent emotions are still there, churning beneath her quiet exterior. Indeed, nature is equally deceptive like that. Here I can see the sun and clouds outside our window appearing so still, so fixed that I can't even tell we're moving. Yet, suddenly unseen winds and crosscurrents can buffet the plane, just as unseen crosscurrents can arise and unexpectedly disrupt what seems to be the calm, orderly progression of our lives, buffeting the balance we think we have.

It's not as if the sudden disruption really came out of nowhere; it was always there, lurking, and when the moment comes when one has to confront it, when it can no longer be ignored, one's belief in order is thrown into chaos. The turbulence that hit our plane a moment ago was part of a weather pattern that was always there, shifting and moving. It was the moment when the plane hit it that we, the passengers, became aware of it. Our notion of a perfectly still sky was suddenly shattered.

Oh, G-d, am I starting to sound like Zach? My own thoughts are now reminding me of how confident Zach was that he would be able to demonstrate J's abilities to his peers. Yet, in an oddly related way, how can I be so certain the turbulence existed before we encountered it—that it was there, waiting, invisible, in the air ahead of our plane? I've got to get a grip if I'm to take care of Sara and be ready to face J and Abram. Of course, my own thoughts are not truly like Zach's.

From reading Zach's notes and monograph, I can see his increasing certainty of J's supposed abilities and the appeal to his ambition that his name would be secure among the ranks of great psychoanalysts by demonstrating what J could do. I can detect in Zach's writing an upward arc of greater and greater excitement, if not an odd sort of pendulum-like oscillation between agitation and the anticipated ecstasy that J would crown Zach's career in glory. As a young student in med school, hoping to follow in Zach's footsteps, I recall being in the Weiss's home the night before the Columbia experiment in front of the Board of Examiners and observing first-hand the way Zach, mid-meal, pushed his chair back, stood up and began pacing back and forth across the dining room, mumbling to himself about the potential to revise.

"What's that Zach? Revise what? What are you off muttering about now? Please, honey, come sit and join the family for dinner."

"Esther, let me be dear! You all finish eating. I'm not hungry just now and you've no idea what I have to deal with tomorrow before the Board of Examiners. Enjoy your meal, all of you. I'm fine."

"Suit yourself then Zach, if you don't want to sit with us—fine, so I'll let you be. Let the brisket get cold—what's it to me?" Then Esther turned back to her plate of brisket and potato latkes.

Recalling all of this only made reading the Colombia transcript so much more painful: the moment when Zach's enthusiasm crashed because of J's failure to show his ability in front of the Committee. Of course, Zach never recovered from that disaster.

Maybe, despite my childhood jealousy of the Weiss family after I lost my own father so violently, *disaster* was the one actual inheritance passed down in the Weiss family? Just as Zach was left to swallow his *disaster* of the failed Columbia experiment, Sara seems to have since then inherited one *disaster* after another of her own, with her miscarriage and her father's death coming within two weeks of each other. All the while enduring the slow torture of seeing her mother slipping away. There wasn't even the illusion of peaceful, sunlit skies to comfort Sara.

I can only hope this meeting with Abram and J might bring all this turbulence to some sort of conclusion, some sort of levelling that the pilots at the front of the plane, focused as they must be in the cockpit, will deliver us to, at least for the time being. Meantime, I see the stewardess approaching down the aisle and, with Sara asleep, I think it's time to order myself a drink and try take the edge off.

2.
Sara Himmelfarb's Unsent Letter to Her Mother, Esther

August 27th, 2018

Dear Mom,

This is the letter I wish I could have sent sooner, when you would have been able to understand what I'm trying to tell you. But I know it's too late—no matter; I want to put down in words what Isaac and I found out about Abram.

To be honest, after Abram disappeared from Harvard, neither you nor Dad ever wanted to talk about Abram. It was as though he'd almost never existed. Dad stopped talking about him at all and you even dropped him from your daily to-do list, just as you'd done when Joshua died. I understand how important order was for you in running the household since the slightest indication of any disorder threatened your sense of calm and stability. Erasing Joshua, then Abram, from your lists was a way of maintaining control and pretending everything was alright.

I remember vividly how you wept for Joshua both after the news of his accident and throughout the Shiva. Yet, after that was done, you never said his name again. The same was true after Abram vanished—weeping, then silence. I could never get Dad or you to talk to me about my brothers. All these years, I've felt so alone—yes, Isaac would talk to me about Joshua and Abram, but not my own parents.

You had no idea what it felt like when I was with you—like some scene out of *1984* where people who fell out of favor with the authorities ceased to exist at all. All previous mention of them disappeared and it seemed they were never real. It was like you and Dad had silently agreed to revise our family history without letting me in on it and suddenly, I was, in effect, an only daughter, and my brothers were just figments of my imagination, or foggy memories that only I had rumbling around in my head. I couldn't erase the brothers I loved and missed. Maybe this letter is the best I can do at revising reality—writing a letter to a mother incapable of comprehending my words, but still putting them on paper as if you could understand what I'm putting down here in black and white. Yes, that's what I'm doing, isn't it? Revising your Alzheimer's away as I write this.

Do you know, Mom, after you got sick, I was actually glad to see Joshua and Abram reappear in those damned daily lists of yours? It was like they had been restored to our family's reality. Of course, I know it was just another sign of your dementia—completely confusing the past and the present—that should have made me sad, but somehow it brought me an odd sort of comfort.

Still, other than Isaac, I've had no one in our family to help me deal with the loss of our baby. When I did tell you, you said that was nonsense, that I was just a girl. Of course, you had lost all memory of my growing up into an adult or my marriage to Isaac or my subsequent pregnancy. With your response to my miscarriage, I felt you had erased another family member, albeit one that never actually arrived, my lost baby—as if my entire pregnancy had been deleted in your revision of my life.

Mama, I'm sorry to be going on like this. I had to get this off my chest and also let you know how I feel about it all before letting you know that Isaac and I not only found out where Abram is living, but now we're visiting him on a ranch on the outskirts of Modesto, California.

Abram has become this guru who heads a cult religion he created. In it, he claims he's guided by Lord Moses, Lord Jesus Christ and Lord Buddha, and they mediate their messages to him through a spiritual medium that Abram calls the Spectral Handler. Also, Abram no longer goes by his given name, but everyone here refers to him as Magnus Pater, or Great Father. So, when we had a driver take us from the airport in Modesto to Abram's commune, I kept worrying we were headed to some wild place full of nuts that Abram had collected to follow his new religion—still, I was so excited to see Abram after all these years, I ignored my fears and looked out at the sky from the car as we approached the commune and saw how the sun was starting to set and the sky was beautifully filled with hues of brilliant yellow and deep red.

When we arrived at Abram's commune, I was relieved to see it was very neat and tidy, with well-kept grounds and buildings in good condition. The main house is a long, ranch-style structure that dominates the area. There are also a series of small houses where the commune members live.

I saw children playing around the backyards of several houses, as well as in a playground complete with swing sets, slides and a sandbox where kids were playing. I was relieved to see that they looked reasonably neat and tidy and appeared well fed. I had read all sorts of awful stories about how children of other cults were treated, having to wear shabby clothes and being abused as well as dirty. These children seemed genuinely happy playing their games.

The guest house we're staying in, a small, two-story structure that's quite comfortable, is just to the right of the main residence. When I first came face-to-face with my brother Abram, after so many years, he was wearing a Russian-style male blouse of dark blue buttoned at the neck. His suit consisted of a black loose jacket, whose tails reached down to the hollows of his knees, and tightly-fitted pants. Complementing this were black leather boots coming up close to his knees. His black hair is now bushy and he has a thick beard. He looks like a cross between a nineteenth-century Russian Romantic poet and the very eccentric French writer of the same period, Josephin Peladan.

Despite Abram's bizarre outfit, his followers here dress in ordinary, casual clothes. Their children too dressed in kid-appropriate clothing. I then realized none of my stereotypes of the residents of a commune led by a charismatic leader pertained to Abram's commune. I got the oddly reassuring feeling that Abram didn't want robotic followers who'd mimic him in dress, but rather people who could be themselves and yet still follow him.

At our first meeting, Abram stretched out his arms in greeting. "Oh, Sarah, Isaac, we rejoice that our spiritual guides have enabled us to reunite after so many years. Isaac, tell us, how was your journey here?"

Isaac, after staring at Abram for a minute, stammered out, that our flight was fine. Then, smiling at me, Abram asked me in a soft, sweet voice, "And, Sara, how are you? Was the trip not too difficult for you given your recent travails?"

Despite Abram's high-flown diction, as I looked into his gentle hazel eyes and he looked back into my eyes, it was as if we were transported to the backyard of our childhood home where we'd played for so many years and so often looked into each other's eyes as kids, both of us wanting to stretch after-school play longer before having to return into our house for supper. I even remembered Abram once suggesting that as he became a more skilled magician, he would do exactly that—stretch our afternoons longer so we could continue playing on the swing set. Oddly, as I continued staring into Abram's sensitive hazel eyes, it was as if they offered a mirror and he was sharing the exact same nostalgic thoughts I was having, while all his wild hair, his beard and strange clothing disappeared and all I saw was the same brother, same hazel eyes, same Abram I'd grown up with. "No, the trip wasn't too hard on me at all. I'm just so grateful for the chance to reconnect with you—you've no idea how much I've missed you all these years." As I said this I fought off shedding tears.

Abram then motioned to a man beside him to step forward. The young man stood at about five feet nine and appeared to be in his late thirties or just forty years old at most. He was wearing round horn-rimmed eyeglasses that appeared a bit small for his face. Also he was slender with dark brown hair and was wearing a white shirt and beige chinos with loafers, in sharp contrast to

Abram's elaborate costume. The young man looked as ordinary as a person could be, save for the fact that he had an extremely long brown beard that actually covered the top of his shirt and dropped down over his chest.

"Isaac, this is Cygnus, whom our former father identified as J and the world knew as William Pierce. Cygnus is eager to talk to you, but first you and Sara should get settled in the guest-house and then we have a special dinner prepared in honor of your visit."

Dinner, in the commune's main dining room with Abram and twelve of us in all, turned out to be an elaborate meal. Abram, of course, was at the head of the long table and we, as his guests, were seated to his immediate left and right. I was happy he put me to his immediate right, it meant he saw me as the first guest of honor and Isaac, on Abram's left, the second. (It's nice to be regarded as first, I must admit.)

The other tables in the dining hall were occupied with other commune members and their children as though at a family restaurant. Again, I was pleasantly surprised to be proved wrong about Abram's cult, unlike so many others, where parents and children were strictly segregated, these children gravitated between their parents and a plump woman whom I later found out was Colomba, the director of the meditation classes, who also taught the preschoolers who lived with their parents on the grounds.

The dinner guests were seated with five on the left and five on the right, and Cygnus was at the foot of the table. Meantime, the children were seated with Colomba at a table beside us, where Colomba kept them quiet and respectful in the presence of the leader of their commune, Abram.

Colomba, I later learned, was in charge of the meditation classes, and also often supervised the children. She had a special magic with the kids, seemingly without being the least bit stern, they all loved her so much, they listened to her every direction, were well-behaved and truly seemed happy, peaceful. Colomba, a young though plump blonde woman who looked as if she had grown up on California beaches, was dressed in a gingham shirt and tight jeans shorts. Both her perfect tanned skin and gentle blue eyes struck me immediately. I've no idea why, but something inside me made me feel like I wanted to get to know her, perhaps even grow closer to Colomba.

Suddenly printed menus were provided for the guests that showed the courses to be served. First course was to be a salad with blue cheese dressing. The main course was to be chicken with mashed potatoes and asparagus. Desert was to be apple pie topped with vanilla ice cream.

Looking at the menu, I said to Abram, "I don't mean to be a bother but, I have a slight allergy to blue cheese dressing. Maybe I should skip the first course?"

Abram waved his hand, "It's no problem. What dressing do you prefer?"

"I like oil and vinegar actually," I said.

Abram then locked eyes with Cygnus at the foot of the table and nodded to him.

Cygnus nodded back and quietly said, "No problem, Magnus."

I was perplexed as to what exactly was going on, then I glanced at the menu and saw the description of the first course had indeed been changed to salad topped with oil and vinegar. Staring at the menu with amazement, I then looked at Abram, "How . . . how did that happen?"

"Cygnus has remarkable talents. I cannot begin to tell you the potential scope of his capacity to revise things and, no doubt, if you've retained one iota of the imagination I recall you possessing as a child when we played in our backyard, surely you can see, as I do, how much of our world begs for revision. Our former father's view, confining Cygnus's skills, which he derogatorily categorized as a 'mania,' as simply shuffling letters on a page in a book, could not have been a more reductive perspective on the potential of Cygnus, particularly in light of all this world desperately needs to have revised." Abram smiled and nodded toward the kitchen.

Suddenly, the kitchen staff emerged to serve the first course; the salad was topped with oil and vinegar. But how did that happen? Neither Abram nor Cygnus had sent word to the kitchen staff about the different dressing I wanted. The kitchen was out of earshot from the dining hall, so now, in addition to not having a clue as to how the printed menu had changed, I was even more baffled as to how the staff knew to change the dressing from blue cheese to oil and vinegar.

Maybe it's silly of me to go on about such a thing as salad dressing, but there was definitely something weird going on, though Abram acted as if all was quite normal as our salads were set in front of us. I didn't know what to think—who knows? Maybe I was just out of it from jetlag and seeing things where there was nothing?

The rest of the meal was splendid. No alcoholic drinks were served in keeping with Abram's no-alcohol rules. During dinner, when I asked Abram how he ended up in this commune after he left Harvard, Abram smiled and replied:

"You should know how I made my journey to this new life. The others here know the tale of course but, as my former sister and twin, we will repeat our history for you, Sara."

Excited whispers rose from around the table: "Magnus is going to speak about his creation story," one guest said to a woman to his left. "Our Great Father is about to speak, shush. Quiet down," a man with a scraggly beard and wild eyes opposite the woman who first spoke said. Then all heads turned towards Abram, waiting for him to resume speaking to me.

"Yes, we wandered the length of this land from New England to California as Ishmael did in the desert. When we had a little money, we traveled by bus with no destination in mind except westward. A still, small voice told us this was the direction in which we had to go before all questions could be answered. Along the way, we worked in such places as restaurant kitchens if work was available and we even begged in the streets if there was no work. At other times, we even did impromptu magic shows on sidewalks, of the kind we used to perform as a child." Abram looked at me and chuckled, "Sara, do you remember how you used to assist us when we did such shows in our old backyard?"

"Of course, sweetie, that was such fun!"

"But what no one knew then was that our interest in so-called magic was a harbinger of the future where, one day, we would demonstrate the false and unstable existence of what mankind calls reality, just as our friend, Cygnus, helped us to provide evidence of that truth. Yes, we kept heading west until we reached the outskirts of Modesto. That small voice, whom we now recognize to have been the Spectral Handler, told us that we must wander the countryside and fast while praying to the sky, the hills and the streams for the divine was in each of these, just as we would later understand how the divine resides everywhere in hidden fires that constantly shape and reshape what appears to be so stationary to us."

Poor Isaac just concentrated on eating his food. I could tell by his shifting around in his chair and occasional forced expressions of interest as Abram was telling his story that Isaac was horribly uncomfortable. I wonder if he is still troubled, as he was back home, that Dad had accepted his patient's delusions and here, in Modesto, it seemed Abram was doing the same thing.

"And so, here we were, wandering the hills near Modesto, and then it came, the blaze of light from above. We kneeled humbly and then we saw three figures in the sky surrounded by red and yellow flames above us and the three fiery figures' emanations converged on a star shaped form below them. 'Know this, below us is your supreme guide, the Spectral Handler who will communicate our guidance to you,' we heard. Then quietly, we asked if we might know the names of these great fiery beings who deigned to speak to us. 'We are Lord Buddha, Lord Moses and Lord Jesus who are watching over you,' one said. 'No longer will you be known as Abram Weiss. You are now Magnus Pater, for you will be as a father, a true father, to your flock,' another said. 'Modesto is your destiny and there you will establish your community,' the last one told us. Then I asked, 'What sort of community?' As they answered us, we lost track of who was speaking to us, but we remember their words exactly. They said: 'You will preach your word to those bedeviled by the so-called real world, as well as those whose minds have been deranged by drugs and alcohol, those false comforts that leave so many numb and lost, wandering in their own illusory haze. You will tell such sufferers they have no need for false aids, such as drugs or alcohol, and one will come to you with unique abilities he has yet to master or realize their scope, whom you will aid to realize his full potential and assist you as you tell those deranged by the world, as well about how, with our help as communicated to you through the Spectral Handler, you can lead them on the path to perceiving the malleability of reality as a means of achieving peace and oneness with all that is abstract—namely, the universe.'"

Suddenly, one of the guests shouted out a wordless cry. I turned to Abram, concerned, "What's the matter with her?" I could see she had her eyes closed and her head was shaking.

Abram patted my hand, "It's nothing to be concerned about. Often when we speak of our creation story, certain companions feel an upsurge of energy within them that they can only release through a shout. Some refer to such a phenomenon as a *cria*."

"But what happened next, after your experience with that blaze of light?" I asked my brother.

"After our experience that started in the hills near Modesto, we spoke on street corners in Modesto, words dictated to us by the Spectral Handler to facilitate our mission, and we slowly gained adherents, not just from places like homeless shelters, but also individuals whom the world would term successful but were miserable inside, finding solace, like the destitute, in drugs and alcohol."

"But how did you get this land and build this place?"

"In the end, dear Sara, it was just one such unfortunate who helped us. Albeit financially wealthy, this man was a spiritually impoverished drug addict, who oddly enough had made his fortune as a real estate developer before falling victim to his seemingly inescapable drug addiction. So, given his professional background, after we'd followed the directions of the Spectral Handler and were able to free this man of his addiction, in gratitude he offered his own resources for us to acquire this property and he supervised the work to put up our buildings with architects and contractors.

At this point, Abram stopped speaking aloud, leaned over and whispered into my ear, while pointing at a particularly tall and thin man sweeping the wooden floor in a far corner of the dining hall. "That is Blue Jay. I'd introduce you, but he is extremely shy and rarely speaks to anyone. Rather, he prefers to remain to himself, but always in close proximity to others while silently occupying himself with menial tasks for the commune."

No one at the table said a word while Abram was speaking. A few guests were weeping. I didn't know what to say after that except, "I'm just so glad to be with you. I've felt so alone, missed you so much."

Abram looked at me and Isaac, "You are both with us now, dear Sara and Isaac. Fear or sadness need never be the Master of our days anymore. Just as we played peacefully in the backyards of our homes as children, we can now, as adults, be at peace here, in the backyards of our lives."

After dinner, Abram squeezed my hands while looking into my eyes deeply, as if he were reading there all that had happened to me since the last time I visited him at Harvard so many years earlier.

Just as we were starting to leave and head to the guesthouse, Abram called out to me, "Sara, do you want to join Colomba's Women's Meditation group tomorrow morning?"

"Sure, when and where?"

"Meet here, in the main building at 9 A.M."

"Great. I'll be here. Thanks so much and goodnight." Then, feeling possessed, I ran back to the table and hugged my brother for so long that it seemed I didn't want to let go of him for fear that if I did I might lose him again as I had so many years ago. Then I noticed Isaac was standing beside us, as was Abram, who then let go of me and embraced Isaac briefly.

In the guesthouse, we went to bed soon after dinner, but I woke up early. With Isaac still asleep, I started writing this letter that I'll never send you. Mama, I know you're a ghost, and there's no revising that reality as easily as a type of salad dressing I might want—though, I still don't get it. How did the dressing on the printed dinner menu change last night—did I just imagine that? But how on earth did the staff know to change the dressing to my oil and vinegar?

Well, I still figure maybe I'm just confused about it all, not thinking clearly because I didn't sleep enough on the plane, had jetlag and was overexcited about seeing Abram after so many years apart—who wouldn't be confused and why make such a fuss over such a silly thing as salad dressing? I just thank G-d I'm able to be with my brother again, even if this place is kind of crazy—I don't care about anything except being with Abram, or Magnus, or whatever the hell he wants to be called these days.

Hell, I'm even ready, actually looking forward to this meditation class Abram suggested that I have to go to soon. He said Colomba leads the class and I couldn't help but notice her last night, look at her often over dinner. She truly seemed so at peace, serene I might almost say—though I know that's a highfalutin word, there seemed nothing phony about her. I think I'll be able to trust her and try to relax and enjoy her meditation class.

Much, much love, Mom—not that you'll ever know it or not,

Sara

3.
Post Scriptum to Sara Himmelfarb's Letter to Her Mother

August 28th, 2018

P.S. Mom, I attended the meditation class this morning that Abram recommended last night. Meantime, as I set off for my meditation class, I saw and heard Abram leading Isaac by the arm to, as he put it, "a unique confluence of spinning shakras," that would occur as they met with this mysterious Cygnus character that Dad had treated and who was now Abram's disciple.

The meditation class, which began at 9 A.M., was held in a small room with three windows facing out. Looking at Colomba, the teacher, I realized, despite her slight plumpness, or rather Rubenesque figure, she was definitely attractive. I couldn't help but wonder how close she, and a number of Abram's other female disciples, actually were to Abram/Magnus/my brother/your son/ their leader?

Once I let go of this distracting thought however, and focused on Colomba's soothing voice as she took us through a thirty-minute directed meditation, I was able to become more relaxed than I've been since we both lost Dad and I lost my baby. After that, I realized I was actually feeling more in touch with myself in a positive way.

Then Colomba had us all move to sit on the floor behind a very low table. On the table, in front of each of us, was a lit candle, a copper bowl, a small sheet of rice paper and a pen. There were about twelve of us there.

Once we were all seated at the table, Columba instructed us: "Now think long and carefully; look deeply within yourselves, then take your pen and write down in four words something you wish were true."

I thought hard on what I wanted to write down and how I could put it in four words.

"Find what you truly wish to be true," Columba continued instructing us, "find those four words that express that authentic and genuine desire. When you find them, write the words on the piece of paper, look at your four words for a few moments then take the paper, light it on fire with the candle and be careful as you put the burning paper in the bowl."

Through my eyelids, I could see the yellow and red shadows of the flickering candle and thought how everything I thought was solid was not, was vulnerable to flame.

"When your paper has burned," Colomba concluded, "close your eyes again and think of those words you consigned to the flames, think how you're causing a transition of thought from the written word out to the world through the dissolution of fire."

As I watched my piece of paper ignite, I watched it dissolving and becoming malleable as it combusted, crinkled, folded into itself, language, four words, now merely charred remnants for the continuum.

After we'd all done as Colomba told us and I'd closed my eyes, slowly, I sensed the words I'd written and then burned had somehow taken shape inside me.

Death Yields to Life

As I concentrated on those words, I saw sparkling lights, like little stars, lifting off the piece of paper I'd written on, amid many strange shifting shades of floating illuminated fragments of red ash, the largest of which suddenly struck me as resembling a star. This star, the red, bright against the night, the ash became larger and larger until I saw it as a baby in the midst of the red ash ascending. This baby, my baby, opened sparkling eyes and said, "yes," as if he were in the room with me. "Do not fear," the baby assured me—the baby I'd lost. Then I started trembling and found I was breathing rapidly, almost beginning to hyperventilate.

I felt a bit dizzy like a panic attack was coming on. Somehow though, Colomba sensed how upset I was, kneeled down, hugged me, kept stroking my hair and whispering, "No, no, this is good, good. You're fine. Everything is as it should be. It's all right. It's all true. It's how we heal ourselves."

4.
Diary of Isaac Himmelfarb

August 28th, 2018

I met Abram and Cygnus in the front room of the ranch house while Sara went off to the meditation class. Then Abram escorted us into the conference room and pointed to the objects on the table. There was a coffee cup which was filled with water. To the right of that was a purple and white orchid. The last item was a plate of roast chicken.

As I looked about the room and at the objects on the table, I couldn't help worrying, as I had been since our first dinner with Abram, that just as his father Zach had been viewed by the Columbia Examining committee as enabling J's delusions, Zach's son, Abram, was now following in his father's footsteps more than ever—enabling and, in fact, enthusiastically encouraging J, or even urging J to welcome, embrace and pursue his delusions further.

Abram gestured to the middle chair at the table, inviting me to sit down, which I did, then he and Cygnus seated themselves on either side of me.

"Isaac, we want you to take a sip out of the coffee cup and tell us what you taste," Abram directed me, waving his hand in the air toward the coffee cup.

I did so and said, "I taste only lukewarm water."

"Alright, touch the flower now and tell us about it."

"Well, nothing odd here, it has that slightly waxy feel of an orchid which happens to be purple and white."

"Very good, very good. Now, tear off a piece of the meat in front of you, take a bite and tell us what you taste."

"It tastes like slightly dry chicken."

Abram then handed me a sheet of paper. "Now write a brief one sentence description of each item and then hand it to Cygnus."

That was simple: coffee cup filled with water, a purple and white orchid, and roast chicken. Cygnus took the paper.

Abram then told me, "Keep your eyes fixed on those three items."

I did so though I could tell Cygnus was reading the piece of paper on which I'd written my descriptions.

Then it happened, right in front of my eyes. The water in the coffee cup turned black and I could see steam rising. The orchid suddenly twisted and rose in its vase and became a white lily. Meanwhile, the chicken rapidly darkened and became juicy. One sniff and I realized the chicken had become roast beef.

"Now try the liquid in the coffee cup," Abram instructed me.

I did and the liquid in the cup was indeed hot coffee. Without Abram telling me a thing, I picked up the lily. It was perfectly white, with no trace of the purple and white orchid remaining and its stalk was longer than that of the orchid.

"Now, try the meat," Abram said.

I tore off a small piece of what looked and smelled like roast beef and ate it. Where the chicken before was dry, this meat was now moist and it stained my fingers as I ate the piece I'd torn off. It was unmistakably roast beef. Cygnus gave me a napkin to wipe off my fingers, which I did, as I felt him observing me with a peculiar smile.

I simply couldn't believe what I had just experienced—could it be? the actual alteration of tangible reality? This defied everything I ever believed possible and was inviting me to enter the exact realm where poor Zach became lost! Yet it truly did seem there was an actual change to my sight, taste, touch and smell. Somehow, four out of my five senses had been manipulated, only the sound of our voices, my hearing, had remained consistent. I had to get a hold of myself. Of course, none of this could be real. I was convinced Cygnus and Abram had pulled off some elaborate magic trick of the kind David Copperfield did when he made the Statue of Liberty disappear.

I didn't care what the hell they thought of me. I had to find a rational explanation and so, ignoring both Abram and J, I got down on all fours and felt along the bottom of the table trying to find some sort of hidden compartment that would explain the apparent transformation of the three objects in front of me. I then knocked along the table's underside hoping to find the compartment that way. Then, in desperation, I laid down on my back on the floor to examine the underside of the table completely.

Abram, standing above me, watched my activities with a bemused smile. "Isaac, what are you doing?"

"There's got to be some sort trick compartment in this table that explains what just happened."

After I'd scrutinized the underside of the table on all fours for some time, Abram spoke up and I hit my head as I lifted it from beneath the table.

"Well, did you find any trick compartments?" Abram asked.

"No, but you did magic tricks when you were a boy. This has to be some sort of well-crafted illusion."

"Yes, when we were Abram Weiss our magic shows used trickery. But Isaac, you must understand, back then Abram merely wanted to fool people, while today, we, Magnus Pater, are offering others the opportunity to see how reality itself can be transformed. Indeed, Cygnus's capacity to show that reality is fluid, constantly subject to change, is precisely why the Spectral Handler brought us together."

Getting up and returning to my seat, I looked at the piece of paper on the table where I had written my original descriptions of the objects they'd first presented to me. As I read my own handwriting, I shivered slightly in astonishment, realizing the words I'd written just moments earlier had changed; the language was not what I'd put down!

Where I had written a coffee cup filled with water, a purple and white orchid, and roast chicken, it now read a cup of hot coffee, a white lily, and roast beef. It had to be a forgery. But how could it be? There hadn't been enough time, I never saw the paper leave the table and, as closely as I analyzed the writing, it was unmistakably mine. I even recognized the paper was the same as the one on which I had written my first descriptions. The original had nicks and a small tear on the upper left-hand corner. The paper on which the revised items appeared was exactly the same.

Cygnus, meantime, said nothing throughout it all, letting Abram do the talking for him, while I noticed Abram again permitting a peculiar smile to play over his lips as I tried to find the answer to what I thought had to be a brilliant trick. He appeared certain I would fail, as indeed I did. Utterly puzzled by all that had transpired, I just sat back and looked at the two of them. But Abram wasn't done.

Abram called the front desk and then put all of us on speaker phone. Abram then asked, "Starling, what items did you bring into the conference room before we entered?"

Starling sounded puzzled. "A cup of coffee, a white lily, and some roast beef, exactly as you requested earlier, Magnus."

I knew the items I had seen, tasted and touched earlier, and yet I also knew they appeared to have been changed into different items right in front of my eyes. Starling, however, who was outside the room and not communicating during our meeting with Cygnus or Abram in any way I was aware of, either was in on their game or, for some reason I could not fathom, she accepted what I then saw before me, albeit a revision of reality, as the only reality she had ever been aware of.

What was truly strange was that I felt the original items that had been from some dream, while what was there now had always been there. My list confirmed it. It was as if the reality I knew shifted and the new reality made the old appear imaginary.

Had something like this happened to Zach when J first displayed his abilities, albeit merely with words in books back then? Back home, reading my father-in-law's monograph, I couldn't fathom how Zach had been drawn in. According to the monograph, J convinced Zach that the printed text of his books had been changed simply by J's mental focus, albeit only temporarily. One hundred percent up until this moment, sitting beside J, in Abram's commune in Modesto, I had assumed poor Zach was indeed a victim of a *folie à deux*, as suggested by the Colombia examiners. Now, I didn't know what to think.

What the hell was going on? I came West certain I'd figure out what happened to my dear wife's father, what led to the demise of his eminent career prior to his being struck by cancer. I felt I had to know what happened to Zach, perhaps to help my wife, dearest Sara, with her mourning, as well as—if I'm going to be completely honest—to help myself, having always looked to Zach as something like a replacement father since my own father's early demise. But now I was on a ledge, leaning over, looking down, bearing a distinct proximity to the final perspective of Zach, having now come face to face with the very potential of J's abilities.

"Are you alright, Isaac? Our dear childhood friend's wellbeing concerns us deeply."

I looked at Abram silently, still wrestling with my fearful identification with Zach, my now deceased father-in-law and quasi-foster father, as well as Abram's actual biological father; then I came back to myself, realizing that, on either side of me, both Abram and J were staring at me, waiting for me to speak.

"Oh, yes," I turned back and forth between Abram and J, suddenly feeling sandwiched between the two of them. "Thanks for your concern, but I'm fine; this is just a lot to take in."

"You appear a bit dizzy, Isaac. The Spectral Handler can affect many people in many different ways. Perhaps it would be best for you to rest a bit now."

"I think that's a good idea. Thank you both. I'll see you later."

Then I left Abram and Cygnus and wandered about the commune's property. After what I'd seen, I didn't know what to think anymore as I walked around aimlessly. It had been my sincere intent to tolerate Abram and J's dog and pony show with the notion that after sitting quietly through it, I would reveal its dependence on shared delusional views and, by so doing, challenge and hopefully even eliminate Abram's enabling and nurturing of J's delusions pertaining to his ability to revise things. However, what Cygnus demonstrated to me in the small conference room was utterly fantastic, leaving me without ammunition to fulfill my original plan of making mincemeat of what I had been entirely certain was their shared delusions.

What Zach described as J's ability to alter printed text by willpower was merely, as Abram had suggested, scratching the surface of what J could do. I had come to Abram's compound expecting to meet an individual as deep in psychosis as Abram was, but following a different set of delusions. What I saw, however, terrified me, making me question the potential scope of Cygnus's capabilities. Could he actually be able to alter the very fabric of reality in ways that appeared to set the laws of physics aside in a way any rational person would find impossible?

As I like to think of myself as a rational person and felt mostly sadness for Zach when I read his documents and construed them as demonstrations of Zach responding to his patient J, by losing touch with his own so-called rational self, I now had a far greater grasp and understanding of precisely how and why Zach was so challenged in his views of so-called "reality" and "permanence."

Just as these last thoughts hit me, I realized I was standing in front of the guest house, so I went in, lay down on the bed, stared at the ceiling and continued pondering what had just transpired. I was so caught up in my thoughts that I felt unnerved and could not bring myself to leave the guest house. Sara, who returned from her meditation class happier and appearing more at peace than I'd seen her in months, seemed a bit annoyed that my mood not only did not match hers, but was a hundred miles away from her own serene state of mind.

Sara finally lost her patience with me. "Look, you're sounding as nutty as Dad. I think I want to be alone. You stay, figure it out, then stop bugging me about it."

"Yes, you're right I'm getting obsessed about this. But, I've got to come up with something that makes sense to me. You weren't there Sara. You didn't see what I saw."

"Okay, maybe I don't know all there is to know about what you saw, but please, whatever the hell it was, shake it off and get this out of your system. This place and seeing my brother as a cult leader is hard enough on me, without you falling apart on top of everything else. I'm making the best as I can of things here and even truly enjoyed my meditation class. Can't you just get it together and be here for me."

In the end, Sara went to dinner alone and brought me a tray of food for me to nosh on later. However, soon after she'd returned, she went straight to bed, claiming she was too tired to speak. But, I wasn't hungry. I couldn't help myself; I kept going over and over Abram and J's demonstration that I'd witnessed that day.

I paced up and down our small guesthouse study, then all of a sudden it struck me: quantum physics. This idea has been proposed that an infinite number of possible universes exist where all the possible choices for action and their respective consequences exist simultaneously. Why must the boundaries between realities be so rigid that one reality would collapse if another intruded? What if the boundaries between so-called realities are much less brittle than we imagine?

While I was pacing up and down and these thoughts were racing through my mind, I found myself looking around the room and I then noticed a bunch of folded paper sticking out of the latest edition of *Elle* magazine lying on the desk. I was curious and found, to my surprise, the papers in the magazine were a letter written by Sara to her mom.

I felt guilty spying on Sara in this fashion, reading her intimate and private thoughts which, as a daughter, she had wanted to share, but could not, with her mom. But I couldn't help myself and, as I read, I realized how painful aspects of Sara's relationship with her mom were.

Yet, I was most touched by Sara's P.S., in which it appears during her meditation session she had some visionary experience that clearly touched on the loss of our baby, as well as that of her father. I found great comfort in that phrase that appeared to Sara: *Death Yields to Life*. To me it suggested that there was hope we might yet have a baby and have a real family.

Normally, as a psychiatrist trying to help his patients find a stable core of rational thinking to give their lives coherence, I'd be skeptical of transcendental experiences that defy rationality, but after what I saw Cygnus or J pull off, I had to do a lot of reconsidering of what constitutes rational thought.

But maybe that's what Abram and J want me to think. I'm truly beginning to question whether coming to Modesto and staying at Abram's commune was ever a good idea from the get-go. Of course, I'm happy for dear Sara that she has this chance to reconnect with her brother, despite his eccentricities, however, while this stay at Abram's commune might offer something positive for my wife, if I'm starting to be at all tempted to entertain the notions Zach did, I've got to get my goddam bearings straight. Given the overwhelming evidence in psychiatric literature that the atmosphere of a place can profoundly impact even the most rational, our staying in the confines of Abram's commune as long as we have already could actually already present a severe risk.

Of course, I suppose Sara's meditation classes with Colomba are harmless enough and so she may very well be safe, but I fear my dealings with Abram and J may quite likely present a very real threat to the stability of my own thinking. Bottom line: the sooner we leave this place, the better.

5.
P.P.S. to Unsent Letter Sara Wrote to Her Mother

August 30th, 2018

P.P.S.: Colomba is a remarkable woman in the ways she gets her students, like me, to delve deeply within ourselves and bring out our hidden fears and hopes. I had another meditation class with her today. There's something soothing and reassuring about her smile and her calm, soft manner of speaking that puts me at ease.

The setting was the same as before, but this time, instead of immediately launching into her meditation exercise, she clasped her hands together, elbows out and chanted:

Oh spirits above, below, weaving though all of us,
Grant us the calm to be one within your streams
Of light, water and fire, be one with your dreams
And free us of our fears that we end as mere dust.

Then Colomba opened her eyes and said: "Today, our exercise is going to be a bit more difficult than our last. This time, I want all of you to concentrate on something you truly need, but this time I want you to distill your thoughts to just one word, with punctuation like an exclamation point or question mark if needed. Stare at the candle a moment, then close your eyes while thinking of what you truly need as intensely as you can. When you are ready, write the word down, then carefully burn it in the bowl. While it burns and the paper yields to ash and smoke and then your written thought gives way to the ethereal, the answer to your need will take form through the grace of the Spectral Handler."

I did as Colomba instructed. I could see through my closed eyelids again the fluctuating reds and yellows of the flame moving and flowing and blending like the streams described by Colomba in her chant. Then, as I tried to follow Colomba's instruction to think about what I truly need, the last words from my first meditation came vividly back to me: *Death Yields to Life*. Also, that vision of the baby surrounded by sparkling stars and reddish skies came again, but I could tell this was a different child than the first, which I felt was the baby I'd lost. Was this the baby I'm meant to have? The word came to me immediately.

I opened my eyes and wrote down: *baby?* Then, I carefully set fire to the paper and put it in the bowl. Even with my eyes closed, I saw the turmoil of the shadows of yellow and red from the burning paper and the candle. What was the true face of what I accepted day to day as real, I wondered as I listened to the quiet crackle of the paper burning? One moment a piece of paper is paper; the next moment, that piece of paper can change to ash. But, what else changes that's not physical?

Since losing my baby, I've fought with my fear that I'll never be able to have a child, never be a mother, but might that troubling part of me be able to change?

Who knows? Maybe I might have a healthy child one day. But if it's not meant to be, perhaps I'll find peace whatever happens or doesn't happen. I'd written *baby?* and then burned it, and in the simple burning of that piece of paper, I now felt like I'd a new internal glimpse of how the physical objects in front of me, those that I'd always regarded as solid, often might not be.

It now struck me that perhaps I exist in a world that might often be vulnerable to change and transformation. Oddly, even as these thoughts hit me, instead of frightening me, I felt a great sense of calm. Instead of feeling stuck in a sad place, as I'd felt for so long, I now felt more positively that perhaps I could move ahead in my life, as changeable as it is or isn't. Looking at the ash that a moment earlier had been paper, I realized I'd trapped myself for years in my mistaken idea that things had to be stable, had to be forever fixed in one way, and change was something to fear.

And then the name came to me: Cygnus, Daddy's former patient. Wasn't the whole controversy around him something about his supposedly being able to *change* things the world accepts as unchanging? Daddy bought his patient's belief in being able to *change* things—and now, by this bizarre quirk of fate, his patient lives with Abram—this strange guy who they seem to believe can *change* things.

The jury is out on that, but all I know, Mom, is that everything I'm experiencing here at Abram's commune has given me hope about trying to have a baby again. Just because I had the one miscarriage doesn't mean my luck might not *change* with another pregnancy. I've got to talk to Ize and find out if, hopefully, he'll agree with me to try again.

6.
Poster at Bus Stop in Downtown Modesto, CA

WRESTLING WITH DEMONS?

YOU ARE NOT ALONE!

OVERCOME DRUG AND ALCOHOL DEPENDENCY NOW.

COME TO THE COMMUNE OF MAGNUS PATER!

FIND A HOME TO HEAL WITH OTHERS WHO'VE FOUND MEANING IN A SEEMINGLY MEANINGLESS WORLD.

MEETINGS DAILY.

209-521-6589

FOR SCHEDULE OF SESSIONS

7.
Isaac's E-mail to His Analyst

September 9th, 2018

Urgent Communication

isahimmd@yahoo.com

To: betrandj@gmail.com

Dear Bertrand,

As we both know, it is a requirement that every analyst have his or her own analyst, but never before have I seen the prudence of this as much as I do now. I know and am grateful we've been doing our Skype sessions while I'm here in Modesto but, events are such that I couldn't wait till our next Skype session, next week, to relay what happened here today.

As I've already conveyed to you, Sara wants to try have a baby again, which I am very happy about, but this requires removal of her IUD as soon as possible if we are to start trying immediately, which Sara urgently wants and is—I'm happy to report—excited about. To this end, we contacted her OBGYN, Dr. Burkhardt, back home and got a referral to an OBGYN here in Modesto and went to see her today.

Since we came West to her brother's commune and Sara started participating in daily meditation sessions, she has stopped drinking entirely and, with the prospect of trying for a baby, I have never seen her happier.

However, one worrisome thing for us remains. Namely, the small fibroid tumor Dr. Burkhardt found back when Sara was pregnant before. The doctor here in Modesto, Dr. Katherine Nielsen (who Dr. Burkhardt referred us to), after reviewing all of Sara's medical records, which Dr. Burkhardt sent her, expressed concern about her tumor as well.

Anyway, today was the big day, the day Sara had her IUD removed, so now hopefully she'll get pregnant soon was our thinking. After the procedure was over, though, and we were seated in Dr. Neilson's office, her words came across her polished oak desk like the proverbial bolt out of the blue:

"The removal of your IUD went smoothly as I expected. But, what I want to talk to both of you about is scheduling a follow up to examine the fibroid tumor that Dr. Burkhardt identified in your file and sent me the x-rays of when she sent me all of your medical records and after we spoke on the phone."

Dr. Neilson announced this as soon as we settled in our seats and then, looking at Sara, she continued. "Dr. Burkhardt noted with serious concern that during your pregnancy, Mrs. Himmelfarb, she found the small tumor and that she had wanted to do further tests on the tumor to determine whether it was malignant. Dr. Burkhardt assured me you had agreed to this, and even scheduled an appointment with her, but when I spoke with Dr. Burkhardt on the phone, she said you'd missed your appointment to follow up on the tumor after your miscarriage and didn't return follow up calls to reschedule an exam to determine the status of your tumor. A fibroid tumor is no small thing to be ignored, Mrs. Himmelfarb, and if you truly want to have a child, you need to take care of yourself if you want your child to grow up with a mother. First thing, it is urgent that you have an X-ray exam to determine if there have been any changes to the tumor since your miscarriage."

Sara turned from the doctor to me, then back to the doctor and asked her, "Are you worried about cancer?"

"Let's not get ahead of ourselves. I'd be remiss as a physician if I didn't consider every possibility. However, the vast majority of fibroid tumors are perfectly benign and this one most likely is as well. Still, follow up testing should have been done back when Dr. Burkhardt first scheduled it. But, better late than never; we'll get you an X-ray exam first to evaluate the current status of the tumor, then, based on what the X-ray shows us, we'll see if we should follow through with an MRI or a CT scan. Finally, if we have to do those tests and any of them raise suspicions, we'll do a biopsy."

"I just want to have a baby," Sara whispered, as her eyes watered up and then her hands rose to cover her face.

Bertrand, the reason I'm writing you now, rather than waiting to discuss this during our next Skype session, is that I'm having trouble living with what happened to me internally at that precise moment when I heard my dear wife expressing her simple, natural maternal instincts and then watched her eyes water up and saw her inability to look me or the doctor in the eye. I confess I felt so helpless at that moment. A baby is something Sara and I both dearly want. Our families have been plagued by the specter of death and loss. Here would be our chance to affirm life in the face of so much unhappiness. But that goddamn word—cancer—had to be uttered by poor Sara in the midst of all our hopes.

Bert, I felt like a goddamn idiot, not a trained psychoanalyst, not a man bolstered by years of professional experience at probing and responding to the subtlest emotional mechanisms of my patients, much less my wife whom I love more intensely than anyone breathing—Yet, in that moment I'd no idea how best to respond to dear Sara. In fact, since that meeting earlier today, after we came home and had dinner, Sara went to bed early and I've been awake combatting insomnia and a sense of absolute uncertainty on how best to communicate with my wife. Here we are, in the midst of this cult-like environment, and, I fear, tomorrow morning, when we are alone, I will find the words stuck in my throat, not rising to my lips to reach the one person I should be able to speak with, to comfort her.

It is three o'clock in the morning now in California as I write you Bertrand, and I know you may not even read this, given the time difference, much less have a chance to respond, yet, other than pacing and tugging at my hair, I've no idea what to do. Writing you, even knowing in all likelihood no response will arrive before I am next alone, facing my dear Sara, still gives me an odd comfort.

But to get back to where this all started, Bertrand, after Sara asked Dr. Neilson in Modesto about cancer and Sara looked away with watery eyes and I felt like the feeblest man on Earth, Dr. Neilson, observing Sara's response, was kind and broke the silence in her office.

"Please, be assured, you are in good hands and I am simply looking to be prepared to care for you no matter what eventuality we encounter. Nothing we're discussing here today is saying you can't have a baby; it's just laying out the safest route to follow given your situation."

"So, I will be able to have a baby?"

After that question from Sara, the doctor tried to tell Sara not to worry, but just to be safe said she wanted Sara to have an X-ray, in order to have a better sense of what we're facing. After that, she said, we could meet again and speak from a more informed point of view.

Before we left Dr. Nielsen's office, she made some calls and got Sara an appointment for an X-ray the next day. Bertrand, I felt both nervous and hopeful, but on the drive back to Abram's commune in our rented car, I didn't know what to say after the talk of cancer. However, Sara was oddly talkative, saying how what she was learning in Colomba's meditation sessions—to let go of trying to control her life, and instead just let her life happen—might somehow, by some crazy coincidence, be just what she needed to prepare her to embrace the best, the most positive and hopeful outlook, rather than the worst of what might lay ahead. And how, oddly, her brother putting her together with Colomba was exactly what she needed to digest the news Dr. Neilson gave her today.

Again, I remain doubtful you will be able to respond to this e-mail, however, Bertrand, I am grateful just to know that you are there and will, eventually, read my words.

Best,
Isaac

8.
Isaac Reads Abram/Magnus Pater's Letter to the Spectral Handler

I never should have sneaked into my brother-in-law Abram's office, but while I am struggling with my wife's fear—the greatest any of us can face: cancer—I have to know more about my childhood friend, Abram. I know Sara is staying in this place largely to reconnect with her brother, Abram, the boy I'd played kick the can with at dusk in his family's backyard, next to my own childhood home, crouching and hiding behind trees.

I know Abram was the boy who, after my dad took his own life, when other kids at school stayed away from me or dodged me in the school halls between classes, as if family troubles or death was contagious, was always at my side as I spun the combination on my locker in the hall, offering a protective, menacing, "fuck you" glare at the kids who, rather than offering sympathy after my father was gone, looked at me like I was carrying some sort of plague.

Despite this history of kindness when I needed it the most, in Modesto, with my dear Sara sick, I could not resist, when I knew Abram was busy elsewhere, I entered his office and, after rifling through the papers on his desk, I found a letter he'd written to his "Spectral Handler":

"Fuck that. Oh Ize, I think my entire family is maybe cursed. First Joshua dies, then Abram vanishes and becomes this strange guru, then I have a miscarriage two weeks before Dad dies. Now I'm standing here about to climb into this huge machine they're sticking me into like I'm some sort of goddamn torpedo."

At this point, Sara was in her gown and approaching the room when the technician appeared and had apparently overheard her. "If you really feel you cannot do this today, Mrs. Himmelfarb, we can cancel and reschedule, though once you're here I urge you to give it a shot. I do these on people all day and can tell you it's really not so horrible and will be over before you know it."

"Fine, let's just get it the hell over with."

Later, after the test, she wanted the results, but of course was told by the technician that he could not provide any reading of the test, but would send everything over to Dr. Neilson, who would examine the results of the MRI and then meet with us to explain everything.

On the drive back to the commune, Sara was driving, not speaking, then suddenly swerved in front of two cars, crossing two lanes, skidding into a small mall where she parked in front of a liquor store.

"Stay here, Ize. I'll be right back."

From her wild driving and tone, I knew no response from me would do any good.

When she returned to the car, I noticed she'd a brown paper bag with two bottles in it. She put the bag on the back seat, jammed the key into the ignition, turned over the engine and drove back to the commune rapidly, exceeding the speed limit, then skidded to a stop in front of the guest house, grabbed her bag from the back seat, and bolted for the guest house without a word.

When I entered the guest house, Sara had already locked herself in the bedroom.

"Please, Sara, let me in. We need to talk, honey."

"No Isaac. I have to be alone. Just let me be."

Standing in the hall of the guest house, staring at the locked door, I felt I could not stop the questions racing through my mind: What happened to our recently renewed love that seemed so strong and now seems so fragile? What happened to the love that had us more intimate in bed every night than we'd been in so long, then talking till dawn, but now, as simply as a key being turned, has been reduced to a love that leaves no more than a locked door between us?

Can thirty minutes—do the math, a mere fucking eighteen hundred seconds in a tube, the MRI Sara just endured, that damn aggregate of seconds—so utterly demolish the love that was holding us together so intensely? And what lies ahead now? Will Sara need a biopsy and, if so, will the biopsy tell us if the cancer is so aggressive my honey might die? We started with the ultimate intimate, loving, question of might we have a baby or not—might new life lie ahead—and now we are facing the ultimate question of mortality—not new life, but death.

Of course, Sara is alone with a bottle—were I in her shoes I quite likely would be the one behind the locked door just trying to be numb, to escape the grim uncertainty ahead.

More than anything else, of course, all these questions, the uncertainty of it all, weighs on us unbearably, sustains our silence, and locks, not only our bedroom door here in the guest house, but also locks the door to that thing called the future, that thing called life.

Why won't Sara let me in? Not just to the physical goddamn bedroom, but to her fears, which I know she is trying to swallow from a bottle. Doesn't she know I share her fears, feel her fears to my very core? But can I really? It is not my body that might be assaulted with a deadly growth. Just writing those words makes me realize how alone she must feel and why the door between us must be locked, however much I might wish it were otherwise.

After pacing outside our bedroom in the guest house, searching the narrow and crowded hallway of my heart for an answer as to how best to help my dear Sara, it seemed the best answer, for now, is to leave her alone. As for me, it leaves me scribbling syllables on paper that amount to nothing—cannot help Sara, cannot help us—leaves all unchanged, left to a fate we've yet to face.

10.
Cygnus's Meditation (2018)

September 22, 2018

Magnus has left me in a darkened room at a desk with only a candle for illumination. He gave me some sheets of paper, a pencil and simple instructions as to how I was supposed to meditate and write down every detail of this experience for him to review later.

"Stare at the candle for a minute, close your eyes and think on the play of light within your eyes. Then, write down whatever you have perceived."

I wait until he leaves then proceed with the exercise. The glare of the candlelight against my eyes gives rise to a constellation of yellow and red stars. I close my eyes and perceive bursts of soft red light like stars exploding. At first, I'm breathing heavily and perspiring, wondering if I'll be able to write anything down about this. The lights I perceive with eyes opened, closed or blinking appear to present a universe in chaos out of my ability to make sense of it.

Yet, I open my eyes and stare at the blank sheets of paper before me. For a moment, I see the play of lights on the paper, bursts of yellow and red, a result of staring at the candle. After a moment of hesitation, I realize I had to transfigure this jumble into the concision of words, seek out form and order from disorder.

My hand went to the page and, despite Magnus's instructions, I eventually found the words on the paper that are written above. Then, taking a fresh sheet of paper and staring at its blankness, I watched myself write: *Dr. Zachary Weiss*.

I noticed his name rising up from the page in wispy streams and taking form, changing from the floating letters of his name to an actual ghostly figure of Zach standing beside his desk, but hovering slightly above me, looking down at me with an odd expression. I sense the pain he must have felt when our experiment failed at Columbia, as well as the cancer that ultimately killed him.

I wanted to shout out: "We didn't fail; you were right about what I could do. If only we'd been given a second chance, I know we'd . . ." but then it occurred to me, looking into that ghost's sad eyes, the experiment had to fail. If it had succeeded, despite our best intentions, our lives would have gone in even darker ways than either of us could have anticipated.

Though as it ended up our lives were ruined in different ways by the experiment's failure, what evil uses might my talent have been exploited for if we'd succeeded and knowledge of this got out into the larger world? It doesn't take a conspiracy theorist to figure how some branch of the government, like the CIA, would have gotten wind of this and I'd be quite likely abducted and disappear into some dark hole as they sought to replicate my Logokenetic skill for their own ends. As the candle I stare at continues to present to me Dr. Weiss's ghostly figure, I see him close his eyes and nod in agreement, as though he'd just read everything I've written here.

Then, Dr. Weiss's ghostly form began to dissolve into particles of light that drifted upward. When I look up, the ceiling of the room is no longer there, but rather a vast darkness intersected by a curving, wavering line of brilliant white light resembling the Aurora Borealis. The light particles that had formed the image of Dr. Weiss drifted upward into this line of light and disappeared.

Almost immediately other particles of light emerge from the white band and drift down to another blank page. I see words starting to take shape: I then concentrate on the blank pages left on the desk where the slightest shadowy glimpses of words were just starting to appear.

Now, out of the blue, entirely unexpectedly, a bright burst of yellow light appears to my right. Out of this light a black figure emerges which, as it approaches me, I can see is Dr. Weiss's son-in-law, Isaac. He appears oddly translucent and I notice light particles rising and falling on him. I hear him say hello in an oddly distant voice, then see his friendly smile as he asks if he might have these pages I was still writing on.

I stop writing, look up at him and reply that he can have them, but I need just a moment to finish what I was writing. I'm not sure why, without hesitation, I knew I'd hand these pages, even with the words I'm writing this very moment, to Isaac. After I finished my last sentence, which Isaac might soon be reading somewhere, I handed the pages to him.

Then I see Isaac leaving, retreating into the bright light from where he entered. But after he is gone, I see the pages I thought I handed Isaac are still here, in front of me on the desk, and I am still writing at this very moment.

As soon as Isaac was gone, the light went out and I was back where Magnus had initially left me to meditate, in the dimly lit room at the desk with only the candle for illumination, the pages and the pencil, but now I wonder, with no awareness of my own, if I somehow edited my own writing with my thoughts in this darkened room, with the candle as my only witness?

But now I stand up and walk toward the window in the room and in the fuzzy reflection of myself from the candlelight, it seems the image in the window is not me, but rather it is Zach, complete with his usual grey flannel pants, herringbone jacket and horn-rimmed glasses, staring intently at himself.

After a moment, he returns to my desk where his son, my Master, Magnus Pater, instructed me to meditate and write. Though I know it is me in the herringbone jacket and squinting behind the horn-rimmed spectacles, I feel Zach taking over as he turns to a blank page and begins writing:

Excerpt from *The Revisionist: A Case of Logokinesis Mania*
Dr. Zachary Weiss

Looking back on J's case now that, per the committee's directive, I no longer treat J— although I still loathe that asshole Brennan, I even vividly recall how he seemed to be smirking at me as we all left at the end of the meeting and how I wanted to wipe that idiotic expression off his face with my fist—I am now trying to do better at having distance from J's case, though I miss him horribly and worry for him constantly.

After all, if one looks at the horrible history of much of the twentieth century, maybe J's condition was shared in different negative ways among many of the past century's worst political monsters: Hitler, Stalin, Mao, Pol Pot and others. They all seemed to have the same manipulative power to make people believe in the most fantastic drivel, deriving from their ideal edits or revisions of history, with the most horrendous results—gulags, gas chambers, lime pits, killing fields—all while trying to execute their edited visions. I can only hope J has ended up in caring hands, is doing well and learning to exercise his powers for the good of mankind, not dark inclinations that might still lurk within him from his past.

What is this? It looks like an excerpt from a monograph Dr. Weiss was writing about my case. But Magnus told me that, according to Isaac, Dr. Weiss had destroyed all the material referring to my case in a big bonfire. So how did my hand pick up Zach's pen? Did Zach's excerpt, despite being burnt, come to me from having temporarily inhabited Zach's spirit? Is this what the Spectral Handler wanted me to see—that editing humanity on a massive scale can kill thousands, even millions—that staggering responsibility comes with the power to edit or revise, which perhaps would be best not exercised at all.

Now, with Zach gone, alone with the candle, pencil and paper, a silent cascade of multicolored light particles rushes down. The particles coalesce slowly and then I recognize her: Sara, Sara Himmelfarb, the one my Master refers to as his "former sister."

She is sheathed in veils of shimmering, overlapping folds of red, brown and green. Her face, though, is unveiled and her long, brown hair is flowing backwards in the night's breeze. I can see stars gleaming at the edges of her hair and realize, looking into Sara's dark eyes, I also see that she is holding a deep pain within, yet wishes nothing more than to be a vehicle for life.

I have this intense feeling of the potential product of the love between Isaac and Sara, its capacity for healing, warming the community Magnus has built for us all via this life within Sara, who my Master merely calls his "former sister," but she clearly means so much more to him.

Oh Glorious Mother! Whether it's my Master's "former sister" or some convoluted fantasy of some Mother Nature, as the candle dwindles and the last of the melting wax spills over the old wooden table, I now finally feel at home, at peace like nowhere else I've ever been in the world—not at this table, not in this room, but in my skin, in my universe.

Before me, in the candlelight, I see pages of writing in my own hand, even though I feel certain I'd written only "Dr. Zachary Weiss." Who the fuck wrote these pages? I feel deep in my heart's core that I must show them to Isaac. I don't know what response he will provide that might offer insight to these scribbled pages or if they will add depth and dimension to my experience, however, I feel as if these words are not even in my own hand and, if anyone might offer a glimpse of what's behind these syllables, it's Zach's apprentice and son-in-law, Isaac.

But, of course, I must ask my master, Magnus Pater, before I show this to Isaac. For the moment though, I am enjoying the glow, the flickering of the candle at its deep end, just as I feel a oneness now leaving these words, my thoughts, my syllables flickering peacefully on their own, at their own end.

Might it be that I do not own words or own thoughts? Might the malleability of words on a page, which is as natural as breathing or walking for me, but seems so unfathomable to others, merely be the result of my so-called "editing capacity" in a physical demonstration from the powers of the Spectral Handler? Why can't He direct my hand in a way that others in the highbrow world of the "editorial community" find difficult to accept?

As I watch the candle dwindle to its last flicker, the stunning yellow shiver of the light I've been permitted to observe, I care not what others think of what I've been led to in the shiver of the candle's flicker. I know Magnus Pater has led me to the territory of ultimate insight, and all others who cannot comprehend this may be left to drift in the wind, where so much wanders and comes to naught.

12.
The Diary of Isaac Himmelfarb

October 10th, 2018

After all the goddamn tests—the MRI and finally the biopsy—then waiting in terrified limbo for the lab analysis and final report from the pathologist, we now have the goddamn results. In hindsight, I must confess I was the one terrified while we were waiting, not Sara, who was different after her night of seclusion, walking through each life-and-death medical test as if none of it was quite real to her. After the biopsy was done, Sara hardly showed any response, but simply asked if we could leave.

In Dr. Neilson's office today, another doctor, a short, heavy-set man with thick eyeglasses, in a white lab coat, was present when Dr. Neilson announced the results of the biopsy: "It seems your growth began as uterine cancer, but I'll let Dr. Posner give you the specifics. For my part, I've already called a prescription for a pain medication for you to our local pharmacy and arranged to have it delivered to your brother's commune, where you're staying. Here's some guidelines you should read for the oxycodone I've prescribed. Now, I'd like you to hear from Doctor Posner here, who has far greater expertise than I. In fact, he is a nationally respected expert and the head of oncology at our clinic. I have given him your file and he has already reviewed the current status of your cancer."

I looked at Sara, who was holding the sheet of paper about

the pain medicine that Dr. Neilson had just given her, and realized Sara was showing no emotion whatsoever. It was as if she was frozen in her chair, unable to physically move, much less verbally respond.

As Dr. Posner began to speak, I hung on his every word, but when I heard him say that Sara's growth had spread beyond her uterus and was inoperable, that the cancer was too aggressive and they'd caught it too late, I began to feel numb and turned to see how Sara was handling his terrifying words.

Sara was silent, her face blank, then suddenly in a whisper, as if she was a thousand miles away, Sara asked, "How long do I have?"

Posner, after beating around the bush awhile, ended up saying it could be as little as months or maybe half a year.

Back in the guest house, Sara rushed ahead of me. Just as Dr. Neilson had told us to expect, a bag from the local pharmacy had been delivered, which Sara grabbed, and then she quickly also picked up a bottle of wine, a corkscrew and a glass, all of which she carried in her arms into our bedroom, where she locked the door and refused to speak. Again, I was pacing outside of the locked door separating me from dear Sara, but now she'd just been told she was dying and I was unable to sit with her, hold her and comfort her.

To make matters worse, it suddenly struck me, I recalled that the prescription Dr. Neilson gave Sara was for oxycodone, which Sara now had with her bottle of wine in the bedroom. I, of course, knew it's terrifically dangerous to mix alcohol with oxycodone. In fact, mixing narcotics with alcohol can in many cases even be fatal. I'd been pleading with Sara to speak with me and she had not responded yet, but when I warned her of the dangers of mixing her pills with her wine, she broke her silence to tell me through the closed door that she'd not taken the medicine, would not start it yet, but just wanted to drink, not talk and be left alone.

After that, although I was still at my wits end, I was relieved to know my honey was not risking her life, mixing narcotics and alcohol—or at least so she had told me, but could I believe her? How could I take her at her word?

My thoughts raced, filled with fears, as I paced the hallway outside our bedroom, getting more and more worked up. Suddenly, I put myself in Sara's shoes and thought of the terror she had to be feeling, facing a slow and increasingly painful death as the cancer spread and ate away at her insides. How could she not be tempted to take the infinitely more preferable painless way out, sedated and drifting off to death on a soothing combination of narcotics and alcohol?

Rather than enduring months of agony as one's body is eaten away, with no cure to hope for, who wouldn't choose, instead, to ingest a combination of pills and booze if they are readily available and can simply, painlessly, take the sufferer to a sleep she will never wake from? Of course, I thought, not just my sweet Sara, but almost anyone would most likely choose a painless way out over agony.

But, it hit me—I can't let Sara make that choice! Screw if it's reasonable to consider suicide or not! I could not let my honey go! We still don't even know for sure if there's a chance some treatment might be out there that could help her. Posner is just one doctor. Also, maybe I'm just goddamn selfish, but I don't care if that's it—I won't give up the love of my life while she still has breath in her.

"Honey, you have to open the door just a crack and toss those pills out here. Look, if you don't, I swear, I'll break the door down and take the damn pills by force if need be. I'm serious: Do it now or else I'm coming in."

A few seconds passed as I was preparing myself to make a running lunge at the door with my shoulder or kick the door in if Sara didn't respond. After a moment though, the door opened a crack and the bottle of pills rolled out into the hallway.

"Here, take the damned pills since you obviously don't trust me anymore," Sara hissed at me, then slammed the door hard and locked it loudly.

After that, I picked up her pills and, accepting that Sara would not speak with me again, I put her medication in a drawer of the desk in the living room. Then, I went to the kitchen and opened the large envelope Posner had given us and laid out Sara's medical report across the counter by our front door. Skimming the pages of Sara's report, there was no escaping the grim, fatal reality Posner presented of inoperable cancer spreading through my honey's body—the reality of facing death.

Of course, it was Sara who was facing death, not me. I should have only been thinking of her, yet I could not fight back my feelings of being helpless, useless, unable to do anything to help Sara, and then remembering the only other time I felt this helpless, this ineffectual—the night before my father died. I remember his voice travelling through the walls of my room, where I lay in bed as a little boy with a pillow over my head, trying not to hear his shouting and quarreling with my mother.

I can still see my father's face, the next morning at the kitchen table—haggard, pale. I asked him if everything was okay, but with a curt wave of his hand, holding his fork, my father's last words to me, delivered after lifting his head and suddenly smiling, were simply: "Everything's fine. Couldn't be better. You go to school now, Isaac. You got a lot left to learn yet."

Later that day, my learning more did begin, only it wasn't the type of learning you get in school. As I left my last class at the end of school that day, I remember an odd feeling coming over me, but I didn't know what it was. In the school parking lot, I found my mom in our Buick and, as I climbed in the car beside her, I noticed how hard her face looked, like stone, yet her cheeks were red, like she'd been crying.

"Are you okay, mom?"

"Fine, Isaac."

"You don't look fine."

"Well, actually, I'm not, honey." Then, as we drove home, she told me the brutally simple fact: My father had suddenly died. That was it, cut and dried, a few words in a car at dusk as my mother stared at the street ahead without turning to me, and my father was gone.

I could not help but wonder the most horrific thought of all—would Sara be gone like this, her departure reduced to something to be spoken of in a few words in a car or any other stupid, goddamn place that belittles the magnitude of such a world-shattering loss?

At home, during my father's Shiva, I heard a woman say, "He's buried in our Jewish cemetery? But, how can they?" That remark was cut off by another woman who pointed to me. "Shush! The son is right there." Of course, I later learned the prohibition of burying Jews who committed suicide in a normal place in a Jewish cemetery. Years later, I also found out the funeral went ahead at the Jewish cemetery because my grandfather pulled some strings to get our rabbi to look the other way as to my dad's cause of death.

Shaking off my thoughts of my father's death, I returned to the hall and knocked on our bedroom door, pleading with Sara to let me in and talk with me. But there was no response from Sara. Exhausted with Sara's silence and my own useless pacing, I finally went to the living room, lay down on the couch and was able to sleep for a few hours.

When I woke up, Sara had emerged from our bedroom as if it was any ordinary morning and simply asked me what I wanted for breakfast. I, of course, wanted to talk with Sara about the incredibly intense emotional hardship she was facing, but she made it clear she'd not the remotest interest in speaking of her medical situation, but wanted coffee and aspirin to nurse her hangover, as well as bagels and lox. She kissed me full on the lips and then turned to the coffee machine.

"Honey, I had a dream last night and, screw whatever the doctors say, in my dream I knew I was already pregnant, and the only question for us, honey, was what to name the baby."

"Sara, I love you so much sweetie. Please, just sit down and let me make the coffee."

"No, no—don't move Ize. I want to talk while my dream is fresh in my head and the coffee is almost ready anyways. Just sit still."

"What about what the doctors said yesterday?"

"Screw that, honey. I'm feeling good, had a splendid dream and think we should enjoy our breakfast just now."

After she'd brought our coffee to the table, with a plate of lox and bagels, when we were seated together at the kitchen table, Sara began suddenly speaking of boys' and girls' names for the child she was certain we'd have, especially dwelling, with no small amount of apparent conflict, on the question, if it was a boy, of naming him after her father, Zach.

13.
Sara's Instructions for Use of Oxycodone

October 10, 2018

Dr. Katherine Nielson, MD, OB/GYN
3425 Courtland Drive, Suite 4G
Modesto, California 95351

Instructions for Use of Medication. Read carefully before use. OXYCODONE 40 MG per day. Increase to 60 MG if pain increases but do not exceed 60 mg a day or you run a serious risk of overdose, which can lead to death.

CONTROLLED SUBSTANCE DANGEROUS UNLESS USED AS DIRECTED

CAUTION: Federal law prohibits the transfer of this drug to any person other than the patient for whom it was prescribed.

Can impair ability to drive or operate machinery.

Can be habit forming.

Can cause drowsiness.

Do not consume any Alcohol with this Narcotic medication as the combination of alcohol and this medication can be fatal.

Use the lowest effective dosage for the longest duration as possible.

The dosing regimen for patient depends on their severity of pain and response, prior to analgesic treatment experience, as well as risk factors for addiction, abuse, and misuse.

Your Doctor will check for respiratory depression, especially within the first 24 to 72 hours of initiating therapy and following dosage increases with Oxycodone and adjust the dosage accordingly. Never adjust dosage on your own without consulting your Doctor.

Swallow Oxycodone tablets whole, one tablet at a time, with enough water to ensure complete swallowing immediately after placing in the mouth. Do not soak, lick, or otherwise wet the tablet prior to placing in the mouth. Cutting, breaking, crushing, chewing or dissolving Oxycodone tablets will result in uncontrolled delivery of Oxycodone and can lead to death.

Take Oxycodone every 4 to 6 hours as needed.

Call Emergency Services immediately in the event of onset of any irregular symptoms which might indicate an accidental overdose.

14.
Cygnus's Report to Magnus Pater

October 11th, 2018

Dear Magnus,

I know you wished for a detailed report describing the results of my showing Isaac and Sara everything I'd written during my recent meditation, as well as the poem you wrote, but as things unfolded in the guest house, I can offer you only the report I've written here.

When I knocked on their door, Isaac opened it only a crack and said, "Cygnus, this really isn't a good time for a visit." As I was already nervous about bothering them, I was half-thinking I should leave, but at that moment Sara came to the door and asked, "Cygnus, what's going on? Is my brother okay?"

I reassured them that you, Magnus, were fine, but that you felt strongly I should share with them what happened in the course of my meditation, since both of them were so much a part of what I'd experienced, as well as your poem. I then held out the sheets of paper I'd brought for them.

"If you could just look at this, it would mean a lot to Magnus and me."

Isaac looked at Sara. I noticed how weak she appeared, pale with circles under her eyes, and I wondered if something serious had happened earlier.

"Cygnus, couldn't we do this another time? We're tired and just want to be alone."

"No, no, I wish I could and I hate so much to bother you both, but Magnus said you and Sara have to see this right away."

Isaac glared at me as if he wished I wasn't there at all, but then took the papers from my outstretched hand, as if to be done with me. No doubt sensing the tension, Sara gestured toward the kitchen table and asked if I wanted a cup of coffee.

"No coffee thanks, but just a minute of your time would be great."

Once I was seated in an armchair facing the couch where Isaac and Sara sat, Isaac curtly said, "Okay, let's see what you've got, Cygnus, if we must. Go ahead—tell us how we were so much a part of your meditation."

I said if they read the pages, they will see exactly how important they were in my meditation. Also, I explained that you, Magnus, had been very specific in directing me to show both of them the papers from my meditation, as well as the poem you had written.

Isaac and Sara were seated beside each other on the couch and Sara leaned over so they could read the pages together. Watching them read, I hoped this awkward moment would soon be over. However, my hopes were dashed when Sara, after briefly glancing at a few pages, shook her head and stood up.

"Ize, after yesterday, I don't know if I'm able to handle this stuff. Sorry, Cygnus, but I need to rest right now." Sara then stood up from the couch.

I turned to her, "Is everything alright, Mrs. Himmelfarb?"

"Please, don't be so formal. Call me Sara. I'm sorry, but you caught me at a bad time; I'm feeling thoroughly exhausted. I just have to lie down and not think about anything."

I apologized for being inconsiderate, told Sara I hoped she'd feel better, and simply left it that when she wouldn't be so tired, I hoped she would look at our pages.

"Of course, Cygnus. I'll read them when I'm feeling better."

Then Isaac stood up, took Sara's arm and told me he had to help his wife to bed.

Referring to Isaac as Dr. Himmelfarb, I asked if he'd be so kind as to let me wait in the front room till he could return and read more.

Isaac told me to drop the Dr. Himmelfarb, saying he'd feel more comfortable if I called him Isaac. He admitted he was also quite tired and couldn't promise me any serious or lengthy response to my pages, but he said he'd take a quick look if I felt he must.

"Okay, Isaac, I understand. Still, I can't thank you enough if you'll just skim a bit of this and then I'll leave straight away."

"If it means that much to you, Cygnus, what can I say? Suit yourself. I'll be back in a bit."

Isaac and Sara headed to the bedroom. After some time, Isaac emerged and told me we had to be quiet so as not to disturb Sara's nap, then he picked up the pages I'd brought and separated the pages which contained my meditation notes from your poem. Then he squinted his eyes as he began reading.

I could see by Isaac's expressions as he read my writing that he was startled by what was there. The occasional shaking of his head indicated his skepticism about what I'd written. He probably thought I was mad as he looked up at me with a sad expression on his face and asked me if I'd ever read the writings of someone called Dr. Schreber.

"No, I haven't. Who was he?"

"Well, he was a German judge who wrote a remarkable book called *Memoirs of My Nervous Illness.*"

"What made you think of him just now, Isaac?"

"Oh, I've really no idea, Cygnus. That book just popped into my head as I was reading your writing. Think nothing of it. I'm tired and my thoughts are wandering."

I was so nervous as Isaac read, I lost track of time and then, looking at him, I realized Isaac appeared really disturbed by the pages I'd showed him. How could Isaac accept my account of my meditation, I wondered? Of course, it would go against all his psychiatric beliefs. But, he did continue to read my pages without tossing them aside or telling me what I'd written was rubbish, mad irrational scribbling. Finally, after laying down the last page of my notes, before reading your poem, Magnus, Isaac looked at me and spoke in a quiet but firm, almost detached, voice:

"This is all quite interesting, Cygnus—yes, yes, interesting is the word for what you've written, even or perhaps precisely because your narrative does, as you must be aware, wander and skip about from here to there, all over the place, as it were. How you envision my wife, for example, dear Sara, to be pregnant, seems to hit the page out of the proverbial left field."

The way he commented about his wife, Sara, and the subject of her pregnancy as I'd envisioned it in my meditation, it seemed as if I'd struck a nerve, Magnus, and Isaac was almost protesting too much if there was nothing to it. Then he also railed against my vision, as I'd written it, in my meditation, that he'd taken these pages and already read them, raising his voice despite his warning to me that we be quiet for Sara:

"What is this crap about me taking your pages and reading them, Cygnus? If I'd already read any of this, why on earth would it be coming at me now, like it does, as a mish-mash of your thoughts that I've never laid eyes on before?"

Magnus, Isaac seemed so agitated I wasn't sure what to do. "Isaac, I'm so sorry it seems these pages have upset you. Please, know that I only wish the best for you and Sara and regret so much having intruded as I did this morning."

"Forgive me, Cygnus. I'm tired and, to be fair, my response just now may be due to my fatigue. I really just skimmed your pages and think I'll have to re-read this when I'm feeling more awake, but one thing I'm so sorry to say, but feel I must comment on, is that I do think this fragment that seems to be an excerpt from a monograph about your case my late father-in-law had been working on strikes me as something you've entirely pulled from thin air."

For the first time, I felt really angry towards Isaac. I resented his suggestion that my account of my meditation was all over the place, as he put it, and was truly hurt that he thought my vision of Sara pregnant and him reading these pages, and most of all the excerpt from Zach's writing that came to me, was all just me trying to pull some tricks.

"But Isaac, this is honestly what came to me during my meditation. When I wrote this, I wasn't trying to pull any tricks."

"I'm sorry, Cygnus, I really don't want to hurt your feelings, but to put it as plainly as I can, most of your vision of Sara and me, and especially the words you give to Zach, strike me as something you actually fabricated, whether you are aware of it or not, it reads like you're imagining what Zach, your psychiatrist, might have thought of your case."

"But that's not true!" I blurted. "You don't understand! I didn't make up a word of it. It came to me in a pure state of meditation that doesn't allow for anything false!"

"Well, whatever you say Cygnus. For now, I'm just too exhausted to consider it any further and feel like being alone with Sara and taking a nap. You can let yourself out and I'll see you later."

"Fine! I'll leave. Shouldn't have bothered you to begin with, but Magnus told me to come here. No matter what you think, I hope Sara will read it and it's important that she look at the poem because I think Magnus wrote it for her." I truly hope that wasn't presumptuous of me, Magnus, but I did feel I should do as you had directed me and remind Isaac of your poem.

"Sure, sure—I'll remind Sara to take a look," Isaac muttered, then abruptly turned and headed back to the bedroom without bothering to say goodbye to me.

As I was leaving, I must confess, my Master, I was feeling anger toward Isaac, which I know can only injure my own karma, yet I could not fight my anger. Then, as I passed by the kitchen, I looked over and noticed some papers scattered across the counter that appeared to be a medical report of some sort. Despite grappling with my anger, these papers somehow distracted me and I felt compelled to look through the pages. As I'm no expert in medical jargon, much of the report was confusing, but I saw Sara's name and the words: *cancer and inoperable.*

Immediately, all my anger and thoughts of myself left me and were replaced by horror and sympathy for Sara, and also Isaac. It all made sense now—how when I'd first knocked on their door earlier and Isaac told me it was a bad time and might I come back later, how Sara couldn't read my pages and left, how Isaac responded coldly to my pages. Just as I was digesting the nightmare they were facing, Sara having cancer, and wrestling with my guilt at having forced myself upon them, still holding and staring at a page of the medical report which was shaking slightly as my hand was trembling, suddenly, Isaac appeared in a t-shirt and boxer shorts.

He was furious as he grabbed the page from my hand, shouted that there was no excuse for my snooping into their private papers and demanded I leave. And so, even though I desperately wanted to apologize and share my sympathy, Isaac's intense anger at me was so clear, I quickly agreed to leave and headed to the door, with Isaac's hand pressing on my back. Isaac almost shoved me out the door, slammed it hard and turned the dead-bolt loudly.

Magnus, dear Master, this was the hardest task you have ever asked me to do. Standing on the steps of the guest house, the violent sound of the door slamming behind me still seemed to interrupt the otherwise quiet night as I looked up at the stars.

Sara, in despair, has inoperable cancer. Isaac's reactions were that of a desperate man terrified he could be losing his wife, and my visit only intensified everyone's anxiety. The truth is what it is.

But, then I wondered: *Must* what we call the truth *always* be what it is?

BOOK FOUR

Wherein Sara gradually begins to face her medical condition while in Modesto, Isaac comes face to face with his own overwhelming fear for Sara, trying, but failing, to conceal his actual terror at the prospect of losing the love of his life. In addition, Isaac begins to gain greater insight into the scope and capacity of J's, or Cygnus's, gifts as the Revisionist, as more fully developed under the mentorship of Abram, or Magnus Pater. While the talents Abram has drawn from J spring from the same source within J, which he was starting to reveal when undergoing analysis with Isaac's father-in-law, Zach, Isaac now discerns that Abram does indeed seem to have surpassed his father's work with J. In fact, as Isaac now suspects, despite all his hours sifting through the cardboard boxes in Zach's office, that Zach's monograph may only have scratched at the surface of J's skills as a Revisionist.

However, all of Isaac's thoughts about J, remain a mere backdrop to Isaac's losing battle to maintain a strong external front for Sara, to offer her comfort and hope, while concealing from her his own very real terror of losing her. To cope with his fear and do everything he believes is humanly possible to help Sara, Isaac throws himself into the work of obtaining second opinions regarding Sara's condition, hoping against hope that just one doctor might offer the prospect of some potentially promising treatment.

Nonetheless, though Isaac knows he is doing all anyone can, turning over every proverbial stone in search of hope, he is wracked with insomnia, lies in bed beside Sara till she dozes off, then gets up as quietly as he can and goes to the front room where he paces for hours, till his legs are sore and his thoughts muddled, alternately considering whether there is some course of action he has not taken to help Sara and lapsing into tears, contemplating the nightmare of living without her.

1.
Sara's Third Unsent Letter to Her Mother

Undated

Dear Mama,

I don't know whom to turn to. Today's visit to the doctor was horrible: Dr. Nielson was with that colleague of hers, Dr. Posner—she'd mentioned him before, but I'd never met him. He's the head of oncology and, after a quick intro, he spoke in a detached monotone:

"I'm sorry, there's no easy way to tell you this, Mrs. Himmelfarb, and it's the sort of news doctors dread having to tell any patient, but I must inform you that the growth your doctor in New York identified last year, and which we have now examined thoroughly, has grown so much that it is no longer merely confined to your uterus."

I recall squeezing the arms of the chair I was in, feeling Isaac put his arm over my shoulders, then watching Posner adjust his glasses, which slipped down the bridge of his nose, as he began speaking again:

"Our findings, Mrs. Himmelfarb, are that you have stage four cancer and it has spread from your uterus to your liver and kidneys. I'm sorry to say, the results of the biopsy and all the tests we conducted, without exception, uniformly indicate this is oat-cell cancer, which is extremely aggressive and metastasizes more rapidly than any cancer that can strike an individual."

After that, Isaac lost it, standing up, shouting, waving his arms, demanding to know what the doctors were going to do for me. Meanwhile, in all the commotion, it suddenly seemed to me that the ceiling of Dr. Nielson's office was spinning and I almost felt like I might fall out of my chair.

"Please, Dr. Himmelfarb, I understand your reaction, but I beg you to return to your seat so I can explain your wife's condition and we can talk calmly." Even as the ceiling continued spinning, I heard Posner's oddly robotic voice.

"Screw being calm! You tell us my wife has the most aggressive cancer there is and then tell me to be calm. Hell with that—just tell me the plan. Where do we go from here?"

Mom, at that moment, the words of dear Isaac and the doctor suddenly sounded like they were coming from far away. Although we were all seated in the same room, and I was staring at their lips moving, their voices still sounded like they were coming at me as if they were drifting down a long hallway.

Finally, Isaac returned to his seat beside me and Posner started talking again. "Unfortunately, the cancer is so advanced, Dr. Himmelfarb, there is nothing we can do now." Again, Posner's words sounded in the room as if he was speaking from down the hall. "Her growths are inoperable and still spreading rapidly. Any efforts by us—and we've considered everything: surgeries, chemo, radiation treatments—anything we might do at this point would only cause your wife horrible suffering that will not succeed in extending her life."

I realized they were speaking about me as if I was not there, but I didn't care, I just had a nagging sense of curiosity: "Dr. Posner, so, how long do I have?" As I asked this question, even my own voice seemed to enter the room from far away.

"I'm so sorry Mrs. Himmelfarb," Posner adjusted his glasses again, "but in cases like this, as advanced as your cancer is, we could be looking at months, maybe half a year."

At that moment, I was blubbering, feeling my face soaked by my own tears and snot. I realized Dr. Nielson was handing me tissues across her desk and I was wiping my face and blowing my nose like a child. Then, I felt myself leaving my body.

As I hovered above the desk in Dr. Nielson's office, I observed Isaac's wide-eyed glare as he shouted at Dr. Posner, and it struck me that I'd never seen Isaac so upset before, back on his feet now, shouting, his words seeming to spill out of him in a torrent as he gesticulated his arms wildly. Then I noticed, I could also observe myself from my vantage point near the ceiling, and I thought the me in my chair, looked so small and helpless, not moving at all.

Then I realized there was a lag time of a second or two between when people's lips were moving and when the sound of their voices came into the room from the hall, like a poorly dubbed foreign film.

Oddly enough, I felt calm though, felt like all of this was happening not to me, but to some other Sara, another Sara who admittedly resembled me in appearance and so many other ways, but because she was not me, but some other sickly Sara, although I sympathized with her misfortunes, they weren't mine.

However, even from the office ceiling, looking down at this other Sara who is dying, it seems I now truly get to understand, Mom, more than I guess I ever wanted to, what Daddy went through at the end.

Mama, I'm struggling to hold it together. I know you wouldn't approve, but, as I'm writing this, I'm drinking some wine to calm myself down. Isaac would say "self-medicating" but, to hell with it, I don't care what he thinks. Truth—I don't care what anyone thinks! This wine feels good, so I drink it.

Let Abram and his whole crazy crew come-in. I'll show them "Serenity" goddamn it! And while I'm at it—Screw Isaac! He actually thought I was going to off myself by mixing my new pain meds with the wine so I'd pass away peacefully. It shows how little he really knows about me. He actually pounded on the door and demanded I give him my pills. I did, but, damn it, I was furious he didn't trust me. Don't worry mama, I'm not going to check out, at least not yet. But, damn, Isaac's distrust makes me feel even more alone than ever.

For a psychiatrist, you'd think my whizz-kid hubby might get it that his behavior makes checking out an even more attractive idea. Men can be so stupid sometimes—it doesn't matter how many degrees they have. Will ya look at Dr. Expert Asshole Posner! A maven with the sensitivity of piece a wood.

Mama, I've almost finished my bottle of wine now and am hovering up near the bedroom ceiling, like I did in office today. From up here, I see the sick me writing this letter to you and I'm wondering why should I accept that shithead Posner's diagnosis and prognosis; he's just another man telling me bad shit.

First it was Dad, then Isaac, all of them telling me bad shit about themselves then me. Why the hell should I accept it when these men tell me that I'm dying. Screw that, I'm going to surprise all those schmucks and have a baby. Damn it, I've earned it. I'm going to have a baby and I'm going to tell Isaac, Posner, all the doom-and-gloomers they can stuff it. I'm going to shove this cancer shit down their throats and have a baby and live.

I don't care what anyone says—I'm going to live. I'm going to live and have my baby. Looking down at the me finishing this letter now, I can see the me scribbling to you, Mama, and that me is healthy and going to give you a beautiful grandchild. You'll see. Everything will be great! I'm so happy now that I can see straight.

Much, much love,
Sara

2.
Transcript of Recording from Columba's Cellphone of conversation between Cygnus and Magnus Pater, with Columba's Notes

As I was on my way to see our Master, Magnus Pater, to discuss the meditation schedule, coming close to a cracked door, I could hear He was deep in conversation with Cygnus and, gathering from their words the import of the moment, though not fully understanding it, I thought it wise to preserve their words, perhaps to share them later, so that our community might seek guidance from the Spectral Handler if our Master needs His guidance. Columba

---

MP: These pages of your report, Cygnus, are of limited import to us. The Spectral Handler has already informed us that Sara glanced at only a portion of your writing and though Isaac perused your account of your meditation more thoroughly, he responded to it with skepticism that hurt your feelings. Cygnus, do not take Isaac's words to heart. Keep in mind that even though Isaac is my former childhood friend and the husband of my former sister, Sara, neither has the slightest inkling of the depths or dimensions that our commune's abstract and cosmic views embrace. This is precisely what the Spectral Handler warned us of when we first permitted their visit. Isaac's response is also demonstrative of precisely the small-minded thinking of so-called psychiatric professionals, whose minds are no more expansive than mice's, the thinking that baffled my former father and his colleagues.

C: Your words are of comfort to me Master, though I remain most concerned about Sara and what I found just before leaving the guest house, which I wrote of at the end of my report.

(There was silence for some time, save for the sound of pages rustling, no doubt Magnus Pater reading the report Cygnus mentioned, before our Master spoke again. Columba)

MP: Cygnus, you must know, we also were already aware that our former sister, Sara, has made several trips to a local physician, but not having seen a medical report, as you have at the guest-house, we'd no absolute clarity as to the nature of our former sister's condition. Can you please elaborate for us your experience with the medical report?

C: Yes, just as I was about to leave, as I wrote in my report, I spotted the document with Sara's name as the patient and then I had an overwhelming compulsion that led me to start reading those pages. Suddenly, I heard steps in the hall and should have immediately stopped reading and left at that point, but Sara's medical report, the pages, mesmerized me—I could not move from the kitchen or stop reading, though the steps were coming closer and closer and I knew, at any moment, I would be caught in my unpardonable, intrusive behavior. Again, as I put in my report, it was then that Isaac yelled at me and told me to get out at once.

MP: But can you tell us, Cygnus, what gleaned from our former sister's medical report before Isaac interrupted your reading?

C: Truth to tell, in all humility, I was so flustered and confused by all the medical terminology in the report, which I was trying to skim quickly, before Isaac appeared, I couldn't read it completely, and then when Isaac found me, his anger so overwhelmed me that most of the details of the medical report flew out of my head. As I mentioned in my report, the two words about Sara I recall most clearly, which jumped out at me from the document and have stayed with me, were "Cancer" and "Inoperable."

(*Looking in through the crack in the door, careful not to let my presence be known, I observed Magnus Pater's jaw tighten as he struck a wooden match and lit a candle between himself and Cygnus on the other side of the table. Columba*)

MP: Cygnus, we instruct you now to focus all of your being on the candle, just as you have done in past meditations, but now fully permit the Spectral Handler to divine through your meditation, with us present, any further particulars beyond the one word, "inoperable," of our former sister's medical condition that passed before your eyes on the pages of those medical reports.

(*Still peeking through the crack in the door, I saw Magnus Pater and Cygnus seated across from each other in silence for what seemed like ages. Our Master leaned back in his chair, alternately staring at the ceiling, the candle, and Cygnus. Meanwhile, Cygnus was fully focused on the candle, though his eyes seeming to have rolled back in his head and his eyelids were narrowed to the most tapered squint. The two of them remained this way for so long that I thought of turning off my recorder and leaving as quietly as I could, but then Cygnus, as if pulling himself out of a trance, stopped staring at the candle, looked Magnus Pater directly in his eyes and spoke. Columba*)

C: Most revered Master, I've done exactly as you instructed and, as you said, the Spectral Handler permitted me greater insight into the content of the medical documents I had so briefly skimmed. As to the severity of Sara's condition, I now can say, according to the report I saw, her condition could not be more severe. With the aid of the Spectral Handler guiding my inner eyes, I now recall that Sara's doctors had identified the particulars in their conclusion that what started as uterine cancer had now spread to her liver and kidneys, and is spreading still at an alarming and aggressive rate. Finally, in the dance of the candle, with the aid of the Spectral Handler, I was able to discern both her maternal longing and overwhelming desire to live, despite the bleak medical report, which she is fully aware of.

(*Still peering through the crack in the door, after Cygnus spoke, I saw our Master become another being—his calm, serene demeanor that has always been a comfort to us all disappeared. He stood up, growling and roaring, "NO," then suddenly lifted and hurled the large wooden table he'd been sitting at with Cygnus across the room, against a wall, with such force that the wood shattered. Then he seemed to be looking for someone to strike, to hit, to lash out at violently. But then, as quickly as Magnus Pater's serenity left him, our Master left the room—his elbows cocked, biceps flexed, as he rushed out and burst into the hallway, slamming open the door, knocking me to the ground, though taking no notice of me as he stomped off, down the hall and out of the building. Columba*)

3.
Third Letter from Abram/Magnus Pater to the Spectral Handler

With the utmost respect and humility, we address Thee, Spectral Handler,

In our last letter, most revered Spectral Handler, we thanked Thee for Thy sign in Cygnus's report on Sara, and requested guidance. Looking back on our conversation with Cygnus, it is even clearer that as we listened to the words leaving the lips of Cygnus, we knew he was a conduit for Thee and his talk, touching on both Death and Life, were Thy words, but we now realize Thy sign itself, his words, also contained Thy guidance.

That doctors ascribe a certainty of imminent Death for our former sister and yet her aura most definitely emanates a future not of Death, but of Life, not of Sara dying and being buried, but of Sara living and bearing a child, we take as a definite sign from Thee that Death and Life are not yet as fixed as these doctors assume.

If we are understanding this correctly to be not only Thy sign, but also the guiding principle from Thee, sent to us contained in Cygnus's words, it is now clear how best we must proceed to help our former sister, Sara, and follow Thy guidance, most revered Spectral Handler.

We write now to express our gratitude to Thee for Thy

sign and guidance and, in our humility, we must apologize for our initial difficulty in understanding fully the meaning of Thy sign, and Thy guidance contained therein.

That Death and Life might indeed be viewed simply as different sides of the same coin that can be tossed, perhaps even flipped, is not so easy to perceive. To extend the metaphor, such a coin, once tossed, is not always so easy to grasp, and can slip through one's fingers. But we now gather, through Thy guidance, this is precisely the task at hand.

Your humble servant,
Magnus Pater

4.
The Diary of Isaac Himmelfarb

October 14, 2018

I can't believe that it was only a few days ago, after we saw the doctors, that Sara locked herself in the bedroom for the night and I wandered, dazed, around the guest house, until I finally slept a few hours on the sofa. I'm sure I'll never forget how shocked I was, when I awoke, still numb from dear Sara's goddamn terrifying diagnosis, and Sara emerged from the bedroom as if it was just any other day, in a state of complete denial about what the doctors had told us about the limited time she had left. While understandable, her denial only made things worse. I could barely keep it together and not break down crying. And then, to cap it all, we had that crazy visit from Cygnus.

For maybe forty-eight hours, Sara and I moved about the guest house numb, with her resisting every overture I made to discuss what was happening. But then it struck me: Screw raging about the unfairness of life. Sara needs me; I have to be here for her. I have to be the one to act. The cold brutal fact is that Posner has concluded that Sara's cancer is terminal and inoperable. But I have to explore if there are any possible, *rational* courses of treatment. I know the situation is bad for my sweetie, but every option that might exist must be explored. Posner is just one doctor; there must be another oncologist who might be able to offer an effective course of treatment, unlike Posner's goddamn fatalistic prognosis.

And so I began to pursue the only sensible course of action left to me: contacting Dr. Burkhardt back in New York to get referrals to the very best oncologists she knows. By sheer coincidence, Dr. Burkhardt told me on the phone, the three very best oncologists today all happened to be working in California—one at Berkley, one in L.A., and the other in San Francisco.

After she gave me their contact information, Dr. Burkhardt instructed me to give her a few days to call each of her referrals and let them know she would be having Posner's office forward them all of Sara's test results. Dr. Burkhardt then assured me she would speak with each of these experts personally to request that each of them review Sara's case as quickly as they could. Finally, she instructed me to give her secretary all of our contact information in Modesto after our phone conversation.

Inasmuch as Posner had already conducted all the appropriate tests essential to evaluate both Sara's diagnosis and prognosis, Dr. Burkhardt felt there was no need, and it would actually only slow matters down, to have Sara make appointments with each of Dr. Burkhardt's referrals. Dr. Burkhardt also assured me we should hear from each of the doctors she was referring Sara's case to as soon as they had reviewed the materials they had received from Dr. Posner. In any event, Dr. Burkhardt said she would have these doctors copy her on the conclusions they reached and wanted to hear from us, especially to speak with Sara, as things progressed. She also added, if we did not hear back from them soon, we should call her or their offices. After that, I thanked Dr. Burkhardt profusely for all her help and she insisted it was nothing and then stressed how much she was just so horribly upset for Sara.

The moment after I said goodbye to Dr. Burkhardt, even as I rested my hand on the phone, which for some odd reason I could not let go of, I found my thoughts drifting uncontrollably, then I closed my eyes and was haunted by a ghastly parade of scenes suggesting the absolute worst progression of Sara's illness: Sara on her hospital bed, shriveled, skeletal, shrunken by cancer, hooked up to a web of tubes like her father, Zach, was at the end. Sara barely conscious, her eyelids weak and narrowed to slits just barely revealing her bloodshot eyes staring at me, and me, staring back into her eyes, seeing the light in them slowly fading away. Then I was looking above Sara's bed at the heart monitor as it began gradually to display her heartbeats as weaker and weaker, with more and more time between each heartbeat.

It can't end like this, I thought to myself. I'm not going to lose my wife. Fuck Posner! Fuck medicine! Fuck hospitals! Fuck EKG monitors!

Without realizing it, with my eyes still closed, as my thoughts became more and more violent, my body reacted and my hand, which I'd forgotten I had left resting on the cordless telephone, picked up the phone and threw it across the room, knocking over a lamp and shattering its lightbulb.

"Honey, what happened? Are you okay?" It was Sara calling out from the other room.

"I'm fine sweetie, just knocked over a lamp. Relax honey. I'll clean it up."

Dr. Ira Davidson
Chairman, Department of Oncology
UC San Diego Medical Center

November 9, 2018
Having reviewed the tests performed on Mrs. Sara Himmelfarb by Dr. Posner, I regret to say that Mrs. Himmelfarb's cancer is far too advanced for an effective course of action to be undertaken. Of course, if Mrs. Himmelfarb wishes to undertake aggressive treatment for her cancer we would be willing to see what could be done. Yet, based on her report, I would be strongly opposed to any such measures that would only increase Mrs. Himmelfarb's suffering without offering the remotest chance of any actual cure.

I regret having to convey this opinion, and I assure you I would never do so but for the medically undeniable evidence present in this case. Based in situations as grave as this one, I do believe that complete honesty is absolutely required.

6.
Diary Entry by Isaac Himmelfarb

November 9, 2018

So, that's it. Nothing more can be done. Is the six months they give my dear Sara all the time we truly have left together? A month of scrambling with mavens, the top experts, and all we got is bupkis! Now, we're fucked—stuck in Modesto, in Abram's guesthouse. Nothing has changed except I've got less time left with my Sara.

I'd no idea how much pain my honey would be in, but now that I see her popping the oxycodone like candy, I've a sense of just how much her condition is deteriorating. Hell, I feel angry, stuck and so helpless. Either she's in obvious horrible pain or she's doped up and talking, making no sense, off on her own cloud, sometimes even giggling like a little girl from the meds.

Tonight, just before dinner, as I read and reread, over and over again, the terrifying second opinions, it was all I could do to resist my desire to put my fist through the plate-glass window in our living room. It was only Sara's presence, spaced-out on her meds, nodding on the couch, that kept me from losing it. Later, as Sara and I headed for the main house at the commune for dinner, I continued to do my best to conceal my utter despair. Of course, I have not breathed a word to Sara about the hopeless second opinions I received.

At dinner, I barely noticed what was being served. I think

there were some mashed potatoes with gravy, but that's all I remember except also seeing dear Sara out of the corner of my eye picking at her food, taking small bites and occasionally leaning back in her chair, looking at the ceiling with an expression as if she was numb. I don't think I spoke to anyone, though I know my tears started welling up several times during the meal, and I checked them only with the greatest difficulty.

After the meal was over, Abram came up to me and Sara in the hallway with Cygnus and Colomba in tow:

"Sara, Isaac, we know you both are in great distress and, we are so sorry, especially as we have learned from the Spectral Handler that you, dear Sara, are truly suffering." Here, Abram paused and looked Sara in her eyes with a genuinely tender and sympathetic expression on his face. "If it's not too much trouble, might we speak with you both in the lecture hall and discuss this? Also, if it is alright with you both, the Spectral Handler has also conveyed to us that Cygnus and Colomba be part of our discussion."

Even though I was in no mood to have a conversation with Abram, especially with Cygnus and Colomba there, and a part of me even feared Abram might just be throwing some of his wacky pseudo-spiritual nonsense at Sara and that it might not be good for her, looking at her standing there, staring at Abram as if we were all still kids playing in the backyard, it struck me that Sara did want to be with her brother.

"Sara, is that okay with you, honey? We can do whatever you want—if you're tired we can go back to the guesthouse and you can rest and maybe we'll have this talk another time?"

"Oh, but Isaac, I'd like to do this. Please, is it okay with you?"

"Of course, sweetie. You know I'm happy so long as I know we're doing what you truly want."

Abram embraced Sara then and, after announcing that this was all as the Spectral Handler had divined, he led us into one of the lecture halls, where Abram turned on the light, and we followed him into the room. With the doors closed, Sara turned to Abram.

"Yes, you are right, I am suffering and it is because I'm very distressed about my health. You have every right to know what's going on as you are my only living sibling. It's strange, but as my twin you always could tell when something was going on with me, so I guess I shouldn't be surprised you picked up now that something's wrong. I hate to have to tell you and it even terrifies me just to say it out loud, which I haven't done yet to anyone else, but . . . it's cancer, and it's not looking good." Sara then started sobbing intensely and covered her face with her hands.

Before I'd a chance to move to comfort her, Abram was embracing Sara, holding her tightly as she almost collapsed in her brother's arms. I then shouted out, "It's not fair, not fair!" And then, I couldn't restrain myself, broke down in tears, even sobbing heavily. Then Abram reached over and pulled me into a group hug with Sara and him, and as the three of us hugged each other, Abram was whispering, "We understand; we understand."

After a few moments, I stopped crying and Abram gently released me, while still keeping an arm around Sara as he spoke to her. "You were guided here for a divine purpose and now the Spectral Handler has made it clear to us what that is."

"What's that?" I asked.

"Why, to ease Sara's situation, of course."

I knew Abram meant well, but I was irritated by his simplistic words. "How are you going to help? Sara's got cancer; meditation is, at best, a palliative."

Sara faced me and spoke: "Ize, you don't understand; I've gotten a lot out of Colomba's meditation sessions. My spirits have really improved through her guidance. Of course, I've had my ups and downs despite the meditation but, believe me, I'd be feeling worse without it."

Colomba came over, Abram let go of his sister, and suddenly Colomba was hugging Sara, stroking her auburn hair gently and wiping the tears from my wife's cheeks, then announcing, as Sara buried her face in Colomba's shoulder, to all of us: "I'd be honored to lead a meditation with just the five of us. I'm sure it will be helpful for you, Sara, with all of us offering our love and support."

I looked at Sara and it suddenly struck me, anything she could use to keep her spirits up couldn't hurt, so then I turned to Abram: "When should we do this meditation?"

"We suggest all of us meet here, in this room, at 11 A.M. tomorrow morning, if that is suitable for both of you," Abram replied. "Also, Isaac, we would be most grateful, and it would be most helpful, if you could bring all of Sara's medical reports with you. When all in is in place, we will begin."

Abram was looking at Sara and myself and, after a moment's hesitation, we both nodded in agreement. After a moment though, what I'd just agreed to hit me. Great, more people snooping around Sara's medical reports, but I felt cornered, felt an oddly focused glare from Abram. Then I suddenly was aware that Cygnus also was staring at me and recalled catching him looking at Sara's medical reports.

"Okay, I'll go along, but I'm not sure if bringing Sara's medical reports is a good idea. They contain very technical information, and since none of you are doctors, what's the point of our bringing her reports?"

But then, before Abram or the others had a chance to respond, Sara spoke up in a quiet, but firm voice: "Ize, please, if it will help with the meditation, I don't have any objections if they see my medical reports. I trust everyone here completely and my meditation sessions, since we've been here, have done nothing but help me." Sara, to my surprise, was almost pleading with me.

"Okay, okay, sweetie, if that's want you want."

After that, we all dispersed. Sara and I went back to the guest house. As we entered the house, Sara enthusiastically said, "Isaac, you'll see just how wonderful Colomba is during meditation. She really makes you feel calm and centered no matter how upset you are when you arrive for one of her sessions."

"Sure, sweetie," I smiled, "that sounds great."

After that, we sat up together a bit, then I mentioned it was chilly and Sara disappeared and returned a bit later with a sweater for me, but shortly after that Sara went to bed and fell asleep quickly. Later, I put Posner's report together with the second opinions I'd hidden under my sweaters in the bottom drawer of the dresser and then began pacing, unable to stop thinking.

7.
Sara's Fourth Unsent Letter to Her Mother

Undated

Dear Mama,

I pretended to be asleep a while ago so Isaac would leave me alone in our bedroom, where I'm sitting up in bed writing this letter to you now. Earlier tonight, I spoke with Abram, who guessed I'm sick, and we planned a group meditation for tomorrow. He always has been able to know what's going on with me without my saying a word. I truly thank God I've been able to reconnect with my twin brother, even if it's at the end of my life.

But that's Abram, who does respect me, my mind and feelings. Abram also possesses amazing intuitive skills, and a capacity for true empathy which explains how he has so many devoted followers. Almost all other men, it seems, no matter how well-meaning they might be, seem to think that women are stupid and that therefore they can hide things from us.

I know Isaac thought he was clever hiding from me the second opinions he got based on Posner's report. I also know he meant well, going to the trouble to get the second opinions without telling me, turning over every stone he could to see if there's anything that might help me fight my cancer—having just written that word and reading it on the page, I can feel the hairs on the back of my neck standing up—

But Mama, for all Isaac's good intentions, and his love for me, which I am certain of, it does seem like he dismissed me as stupid when he hid all the medical reports and second opinions on my condition under his sweaters in the bottom drawer of his dresser.

I did wonder where Isaac had put my medical papers and even looked for them here and there. But it was only tonight, a cool evening, after we got home from talking with Abram that, when Isaac complained it was chilly, I went to get a sweater for him and, by accident, I found the hidden medical papers. After that, I grabbed the papers, hurried to our small bathroom, locked the door, sat on the floor and read the reports.

Well, Mama, you know the old saying, "Curiosity killed the cat." I satisfied my curiosity and indeed it killed me to read these reports—all echoes of what Posner already told us. For a moment I felt like screaming, as Isaac did at the doctors, but I stopped myself. It's interesting, at first, I broke down in tears, crying quietly so Isaac wouldn't hear me. But then, truth to tell, I felt all cried out, wiped my cheeks with toilet paper, blew my nose then stood up and looked in the mirror and saw my eyes were red and puffy. I didn't want Isaac to see me like this and guess I was crying so I put a few drops of Visine in my eyes. It then hit me just how overwhelmingly tired I felt.

After that, I left the bathroom and returned the reports to where Isaac stashed them and tried my best to make it look like they'd been undisturbed, folding the sweaters as neatly as possible. I then selected Isaac's favorite cashmere cardigan, which I brought to him, trying to act as if all was normal, then simply telling Isaac I was tired and wanted to go to sleep.

Alone in bed, I pretended to fall asleep till Isaac left the room, then realized I felt a strong connection to Daddy. Also, I realized that I wanted to write you this letter—who knows why, since I'll never send it—Still, it makes me feel good to talk to you like this, as if you could understand.

Also I'm looking forward to tomorrow's meditation session to try to come to terms with my inevitable death. I just never thought it would be this soon. Poor Isaac, he will be so alone.

I want to be with him as long as I can. But it seems clear now there's nothing I can do.

Mama, I love you so much and really miss you.

Much, much love, Sara

8.
Cygnus's Third Meditation: The Prelude

November 10, 2018

"This meditation class that I will arrange with myself, you, Isaac, Sara and Colomba in attendance will be highly unorthodox, Cygnus, for though Colomba will appear to all as the leader, in fact, you will be the true and actual leader of it, not Colomba. The fact that you must play this crucial though 'secret' role, Cygnus, has been conveyed to us by the spirit of the Spectral Handler."

I was puzzled as Magnus said this to me last night before dinner and felt something was challenging my serenity in the role that Magnus was asking me to play in today's meditation and, what's worse, I was and, though I feel better today, still am uncertain if I can do it. But, if this came from the Spectral Handler, how can I question it? Still, as I continued speaking with Magnus last night, I wanted some clarification of what he meant.

"Magnus, I don't understand—how will I be the leader of the meditation session, and not Colomba, if she is going to be there?"

Magnus smiled and put his hand on my shoulder:

"After dinner, when we are all together, we will invite my former sister, Sara, and Isaac to a group meditation tomorrow morning that is going be ostensibly led by Colomba. We will explain that this meditation will help Sara achieve a state of calm as she faces her serious medical challenge and that we will be present to show our support."

"Magnus, how exactly does the Spectral Handler expect me to perform this secret leading role during this meditation?"

"Well, we have been instructed by Him to ask Isaac to bring the medical reports for my former sister, Sara, with him. Once together in the meditation room, Colomba will ask Isaac to lay the pages of the reports on the long table where we will all be seated. Meanwhile, as my former sister, Sara, and Isaac listen to Colomba, you will sit at the table silently, making no physical movements whatsoever, to be as inconspicuous as possible, as Isaac's and Sara's attention will be focused on Colomba when she recites her prayers of invocation and benediction. From your seat, you will have the pages of the medical reports within your view. At that juncture, the Spectral Handler will provide you with clarity and guidance as to how you will silently and without notice take over the leadership of this session."

Although it was still unclear to me exactly what was expected of me, I nodded and we sat down to eat. After dinner, just as Magnus had explained earlier, we joined Colomba, Sara and Isaac and went to the meditation room. The course of meditation outlined by Magnus was met with a marked lack of eagerness by Isaac, but Sara expressed enthusiasm and accepted the invitation to a group meditation led by Colomba.

As we all left the meditation room, I watched Sara and Isaac walking, holding hands, toward the guest house and it powerfully struck me how Sara would be a wonderful mother, unlike my own, and Isaac, I think, would be a good father.

Now, a bit early for the meditation we agreed upon last night, having written these recollections, I remain as uncertain as I was last night as to exactly what I am to do today, but trusting in the Spectral Handler, as I do with all my heart, I feel a positive sort of internal lightness, which tells me that if I let go of my Self and can be as receptive as much as I am capable of to let the Spectral Handler direct me, all should go well.

But enough of writing and thinking. Now I must go to the meditation and be open to whatever lies ahead.

9.
Cygnus's Third Meditation: Finale of The Revision

November 10, 2018

And so, it begins. Sara, Isaac, Magnus, Colomba and I are present in the meditation hall. All the pages of Sara's medical reports have been laid out, covering the surface of the long table, except for a small spot where blank pages and a pen appear before me. We are all seated at this table, except for Colomba, who is standing at the head of the table and has her eyes closed as she prepares herself for the beginning of this unusual meditation.

I am not certain if I am writing these actual words at this exact moment or just thinking them in my head. No one seems to notice I'm writing, if in fact I am actually writing, so I cannot truly tell whether or not I am writing at this moment. Indeed, I must confess, I am not even aware whether or not I'm holding a pen at this moment, so I oddly have no way of knowing how the narrative of the events transpiring just now are appearing on paper at all.

Looking around, I see Sara staring intently at Colomba, waiting for the meditation to begin. Sara appears hopeful, expectant. Isaac, who is beside her, looks distinctly uncomfortable. He keeps looking down at the desk in front of him and tugging at the collar of his shirt as if it's too tight. Magnus, of course, is utterly serene, looking at Colomba, waiting for her to begin, yet glancing over at Sara, for moments at a time, his face almost glowing as he regards her. I get the distinct feeling he no longer sees her as his "former" sister, but now sees her as his sister, his flesh and blood.

Not only Isaac, but Magnus, Colomba and, I must admit, I too love Sara. I can sense Sara, being surrounded by people who truly care for her. With this love, I feel my own fears disappearing; I now feel I can trust to my instincts when the meditation begins, to let myself do whatever is necessary. I realize I am on the cusp of finding out what that will mean. Now Colomba begins to chant her invocation:

"Oh, Spectral Handler, direct the lights of your guides,

Moses, Jesus and Buddha, to heal the heart and body of Sara,

To permit the repose, health, wholeness and peace she deserves

To face her current challenges and past trials and tribulations."

After hearing Colomba's invocation, I began concentrating on the pages of Sara's medical reports to the exclusion of all else. As I focused more intently on the medical reports, Colomba's voice drifted off. I knew she was still speaking, but I soon felt myself surrounded by silence. Also, I knew Isaac, Sara, Magnus, and Colomba were all in the room with me, but I could no longer see them, as they were shrouded in darkness, yet all the pages of the reports became luminescent. Again, it struck me, I had no idea whether I was writing the words that appear here or . . . something new was happening—

I do know I saw particles of light rising from and going to the pages on the table. I wasn't doing any actual reading, just concentrating on the terrifying nature of what I imagined those pages of medical reports contained—all the grizzly details of Sara's cancer. Above me, a white waving line was where those lights were coming to and rising from the medical reports on the table.

Then, I saw those lights rising from the pages suddenly darken and coalesce into a menacing coal-black shadow of a figure approaching me. Although nobody else at the table appeared to see what I was seeing and they continued as if all was as before, I was certain I now heard a low, guttural roar coming from the dark figure trying to interfere with Sara's medical reports.

It was trying to frighten me, this demon, stop me from whatever I was supposed to be doing. But all that shadow did was make me more determined to fight it. I felt myself inwardly calling on all the light the Spectral Handler had brought forth since the act of creation to eradicate this malevolent presence and bolster my ability to focus on Sara's medical reports.

Suddenly, from the waving white line above me, a silent explosion of light flooded down and enveloped that dark shadow. There was a shriek like nothing I had ever heard before, a long howl of intense agony, then the light exploded and formed a bright star above the table that hurt my eyes and yet somehow no one else seemed to notice. Then the bright light disappeared.

"Oh, thou transcendent,

Nameless, the fiber and the breath,

Light of the light, shedding forth universes, thou center of them."

I just found myself chanting these lines from Whitman, praising the infinite spirit of the universe. Yes, there was time for Death in Whitman's poem, but I hoped this wasn't Sara's time. Could it be that Death might just have to wait?

I returned my focus to the papers on the table in front of me. Then, suddenly, rising from Sara's medical reports, and hovering above the table plain as day, I saw in gold the word, "Life." With that, just as the word appeared with absolute clarity, there was a fresh shower of white, brilliant light on the table. I lost my sight and sense of time then—for how long I cannot say. But when I was back to myself, I saw Colomba, appearing more startled than I'd ever seen her, tugging on her long hair and visibly sweating. Still feeling a bit wobbly, like a man long at sea first stepping off his ship onto land, I stood, trying to get my bearings, and overheard bits of Sara and Isaac talking to each other.

"What the hell happened?"

"I haven't the foggiest . . ."

Magnus alone appeared calm, while looking at me, barely concealing a slight smile, mostly hidden in the hairs of his bushy moustache and beard. Magnus then walked over and hugged first Sara then Isaac. After that, He turned to Colomba and said,

"Thank you my dear, we feel that went as well as we could have hoped for."

Colomba looked bewildered, "But . . . but, Magnus, I didn't even finish, at least I don't recall doing so."

"Perhaps not, but the meditation was completed, even if it was a bit of an unorthodox conclusion, Colomba."

Magnus then turned from Colomba and gave me a long and searching look, "We think you understand, the meditation was concluded successfully." I felt myself nodding, though I wasn't quite sure what Magnus meant, but I wanted to believe he was right.

Magnus then addressed us all by saying, "Well, after such an intense experience, we think all of us need a rest before doing anything else today."

Isaac stared at Magnus with a confused expression. "What do you mean? What on earth happened here just now that could in any way alter what the doctors have told us?"

"All we can say for the moment, Isaac, is be patient and all will be revealed. The workings of the Spectral Handler are often quite mysterious."

Isaac appeared incredulous, but merely muttered to Magnus, "Well, whatever you say—I guess time will tell."

Then as Isaac gathered up the pages of the report, Sara said, "What's so hard to understand, Ize? We've already found my brother and stayed here longer than either of us planned. As for my condition—why are you speaking of that now? We're lucky to be expecting."

"What Sara? What are you saying? Are you expecting? I thought I glimpsed a glow in your aura, but then I thought I was just imagining it, though I know the Spectral Handler rarely permits my imagination to be played with. Yes, I knew it—a glow, that's what I saw and see now from your aura." Colomba then embraced Sara and said how happy she was for her.

After that, Sara hugged Magnus and me, and then left for the guesthouse with Isaac looking puzzled and Sara looking calm, peaceful, even serene.

10.
Last Diary Entry of Isaac Himmelfarb

November 16, 2018

I looked over Sara's medical report after that bizarre meditation session we had with Colomba, Cygnus and Abram. I couldn't believe what I was reading. Now the report in clean block print said that Sara was in excellent health, with absolutely no mention of her having cancer or any tumors whatsoever, and moreover, the medical report now stated that Sara was pregnant and, in fact, at the end of her first trimester.

What the hell is going on? Did Abram pull off some magic trick and replace the original reports with one that showed Sara pregnant and in glowing health? I swear to G-d if he pulled a dirty trick like that—to fuck with our hopes—I'd kill him, brother-in-law or not.

That's why I made an appointment with Dr. Neilson as soon as possible to discuss the medical reports, saying that I had further questions about it. It was odd, I noticed that she had a slightly hesitant, puzzled sound in her voice when I requested the visit. I figured she thought that she and Posner had been clear about the grave import of their findings and may have been confused I had any doubts about it.

I went alone as I had made the appointment as early as possible in the morning so that Sara could sleep. Also, I didn't want to upset and confuse her with this apparently different report. I could see how she'd think some miracle happened during the meditation and now she was cured and pregnant. I told her the night before the appointment I just wanted to check some small things out with Dr. Neilson and that she should stay in bed and relax. I wanted to delay as long as I could a reckoning with Abram if this revised report turned out to be the fraud I thought it was.

As I waited outside Dr. Neilson's office, I reviewed the report and the second opinions. Even the second opinions had been altered. I came out sounding like a hysteric who was excessively concerned about his wife's pregnancy and seemed to be obsessed with the delusional idea she had cancer. Still, I wanted this cleared up as fast as possible so I could confront Abram with the real documents and chew him out for his cheap and despicable trick.

Dr. Neilson came out and said, "Hello, Dr. Himmelfarb, how can I help you? I thought we had been clear after our last visit that your wife is fine and several weeks pregnant. Our oncologist, Dr. Posner, did look for and found no small fibroid tumor in your wife's uterus, as reported by Dr. Burkhardt. Dr. Burkhardt had noted her concern about that one tumor, but we found it had gone into total remission. I thought you'd be seeing the OBGYN doctor I referred you to by now, rather than me, though of course my door is always open to you and Sara."

I showed her the reports I had. "So, this is the report from last month you wrote up for Sara?"

She looked at it rapidly, "Why, yes, that's it. I must say Dr. Himmelfarb, I was more concerned about you than your wife, Sara. You seem convinced she has serious cancer and, at our last meeting, in front of your wife, you argued with me that this report is wrong. Your wife was really upset. I understand you went and got referrals for second opinions from Dr. Burkhardt. But, you insisted. I must say, Dr. Himmelfarb, all you have achieved so far is to frighten your wife horribly. I understand you are worried about this new pregnancy, understandably so, but really, I do not know how else I can assure you that everything's fine."

"Look, when I was last in your office, you and Dr. Posner gave Sara and me the most serious prognosis I've ever heard. Both you and Dr. Posner said Sara had stage 4 cancer and it was spreading throughout her body so rapidly, to the extent, that nothing could be done beyond palliative care and her time was limited."

"Dr. Himmelfarb, neither I nor Dr. Posner said any such thing. I think this concern about your wife's new pregnancy has pushed you into an area of psychology you're more qualified to analyze than I. But I'll be damned if you think that I lied to you somehow earlier. Neither Dr. Posner nor I would lie to you about something as serious as cancer. If we were so stupid to do so, for God knows what reason, we'd both lose our licenses, and rightfully so. If I may be so bold, I suggest you discuss this with a colleague and see what they think."

Dr. Neilson knitted her eyebrows and glared at me, telling me she was in deadly earnest and I'd better give up this line of inquiry. I couldn't say a word. I was struck dumb. I had handed her the copies of the medical reports that Cygnus had sent Sara and me off to the guest house with after our meditation session and she had quickly perused them and replied, as she had before.

"Yes, Dr. Himmelfarb, these are the wonderful results of your wife's tests we reviewed together before and, as I told you at that time, you should be a happy man. Your wife is cancer-free and you are to be a father."

I didn't know what to say, how to digest this new reality that seemed to have turned the world on its head. A doctor, a licensed professional, tells you that up is down, that light is dark, black is white, that whatever you had entertained before as the dismal reality you and your wife were facing was false, and if you contradict that position you are to be regarded as mad—what could I say? Finally, I mumbled out, "Thank you, doctor, for everything." Then I left her office and headed back to Abram's commune.

As I drove back, my head was swimming so badly that it was a miracle I didn't have a car accident—I don't recall seeing the street ahead of me or the traffic I was moving through. On the one hand, if this was all real, I had to be happy; my wife, dear

Sara, was healthy, and we were going to have a child. On the other hand, if I was to accept it, it meant all that I thought was true, hard fast reality had evaporated like a bad dream. But how can that be? How can I live with that?

11.
Afterword

November 17, 2018

At this point, though I know as a man of science that I should be questioning what I cannot avoid regarding as my own very inconsistent perception of reality, I am unable to feel anything but joy. I look at Sara, cancer-free and glowing with the shimmer given to women carrying a new life within their own bodies. What if my very sanity is to be questioned—my wife is happier than I've seen her since we ourselves were children playing and I've the joy of actually being a father myself to look forward to—Again, what if, in fact, I'm a prime candidate for some colleague's couch? I don't give a damn! The hell with labels or reductive categories drawn from the latest DSM V! My wife is happy; she's goddamn glowing with our child growing inside her. Let them call me mad! I could not be happier.

Of course, I know all this means I have to consider that Cygnus might indeed have a power surpassing any known to man. Or, did he merely show I was the one in a delusional state about Sara's cancer and that it wasn't Sara who had been brought back to health by Abram and J, but myself they'd brought back to health—do I, after everything, have to accept that this whole business of saving Sara from cancer had been my own mind-fuck?

Or did Cygnus not only change Sara's medical reports, revise the language in them as Zach maintained J could with print on the page, but also change Sara's body, her actual medical condition, to conform with his revised reports? Could it be that Abram took J farther in finding his unique powers as the ultimate Revisionist than Abram's father, Zach, had ever dreamed possible?

And what of Zach's death from cancer, the first appearance of which coincided with Zach's career-ending, professional humiliation after J's failure at the Columbia test? If it was Sara's cancer that J had edited away, and not my delusion that she had life threatening cancer, then why hadn't J edited away Zach's cancer, even if Zach had, at that point, been prohibited from treating J? Or was it only under the guidance of Abram that J had learned truly how to harness his logokinetic skills to transcend the limited territory of a page, to impact on the lives of actual people physically, medically, and actualize himself as the ultimate Revisionist?

If there are any answers to such questions as set out above, I've no idea. In fact, the more I think of the events that have transpired here in Modesto, the more certain I am that I've no business returning to the practice of psychoanalysis and suspect, just as Zach had after his work with J, that I must retire, after my time here with J, quite likely the ultimate Revisionist.

But on the brighter side, I've so much good to embrace in my life now: Sara, my sweetie, is absolutely healthy and, in fact, going to be a mother, just as I am going to be a father after all.

Shakespeare said it best in *Hamlet*, when Hamlet says to Horatio, "There is more in heaven and earth than is contained in your philosophy." Change the word "philosophy" to "science" and put Shakespeare's statement not to Horatio alone, but to the whole of today's psychoanalytic community, and, as I now believe, the merit of the thought will still stand up.

The energy of existence is indeed broader than the narrow pathways of pure logic and reason. In any event, for the time being, we are staying here, living in the guest house, which Abram has insisted is ours as long as we wish, and Sara has decided that she wishes to remain here, at the very least, through the remainder of her pregnancy to have Colomba present to comfort her and provide a meditative state when Sara delivers our child. After that—who knows?

12.
Coda

December 18, 2018

Looking back on the last document I wrote a month ago, I realize I was still digesting the actuality of the new reality—that Sara is cancer free, healthy and carrying our child, with all looking good. I now appreciate how often it is difficult for many of us to accept the goodness of life staring us in the face. Speaking at least for myself, despite all my degrees, I know that that was my experience. I had an odd sort of resistance to good news and a lingering certainty that only the worst that life might deliver lay ahead for Sara and me.

Since then, I've fallen into a happy pattern of walking or actually hiking each day, while assisting Abram, part-time, as he offers spiritual guidance to local kids with drug problems and I offer them counseling. In addition, I've also gone back to reading poetry, a pursuit I loved before my psychoanalytic practice back in New York made me put that private pleasure aside.

Meantime, Sara has been happily busy in meditation sessions with Colomba, and has made friends with other women in the commune, several of whom are also pregnant and have created a women's group that meets privately and shares their unique experiences, as pregnant women, of having a new life growing within them.

Today, while Sara was at her pregnant women's group, I was

listening to the children from the commune playing outdoors, near the guest house, and I was reading from T. S. Eliot's Four Quartets and was struck by some of the last lines from "Little Gidding":

We shall not cease from exploration
And the end of all our exploring
Will be to arrive where we started . . .
The voice of the hidden waterfall
And the children in the apple-tree
Not known, because not looked for
But heard, half-heard, in the stillness
Between two waves of the sea.

Reading these lines, "where we started" took me back to when Sara, Abram and I were all kids playing in the backyard, and Eliot's "stillness / Between two waves" took me to Sara and myself as two waves, still rolling together in the sea of life itself.

Perhaps, via J, Zach reached the conclusion that all documents are, in a sense, incomplete, with what's written, never truly fixed in print, but fluid, flexible, always subject to revision, and there was no ultimate explanation to put all into the ultimate metaphysical order he longed for. Perhaps Zach even foresaw the future potential—saw precisely what came to transpire—of J extending his powers as a Revisionist beyond the page, impacting on life itself, and that was enough to drive Zach into his solitary confinement and eventual complete withdrawal from society when he was struck with cancer, knowing how his advancing the notion that his patient could just change language on the page with his mind had already demolished Zach's career, perhaps he thought if he proposed that J's abilities to revise could be applied to the world beyond books he, himself, would be diagnosed as mad and perhaps even locked up.

As for myself, come what may, whatever others say reality is or is not, the facts that matter to me most remain: Eliot was a great poet, waves in the ocean keep rolling as they always have and, it seems, always will, and, most important of all, my sweetie Sara and I are in love, serene and just waiting to nurture our child with the happiness we currently share.

13.
Appendix: The Song of the Purpled Realm

Magnus Pater

Our collection of poems, *The Song of the Purpled Realm*, written with the guidance and aid of the Spectral Handler, may appear to others to entertain what the world at large might call a sort of didactic mysticism, or more simply put, an odd and exotic variety of syllables marching across the page. However, the epigraph at the front of our book does, we believe, quite clearly set the tone for the volume. This excerpt from a poem by the obscure poet, George Sterling, obviously explicates the intent of our own work:

> Without, the battlements of sunset shine,
> 'Mid domes the sea-winds rear and overwhelm.
> Into a crystal cup the dusky wine
> I pour, and, musing at so rich a shrine,
> I watch the star that haunts its ruddy gloom.
> Now Fancy, empress of a purpled realm…
> Where wattled monsters redly gape, that guard
> A cowled magician peering on the damned
> Thro' vials wherein a splendid poison burns,
> Sifting Satanic gules athwart his brow.

Two poems in our collection that demonstrate our collaboration with the Spectral Handler the best are set out on the following pages. In truth, in all modesty, we can hardly claim having written these poems ourselves at all, as the experience in the composition of each of these specific poems left us with the sense that we only recall having put pen to paper and starting to spill ink across the page, but losing all sense entirely of what specific words we were scribbling or how much time had elapsed as we sat at our desk, then, as if driven by some external force, we lifted our pen in each case only to see the page covered with a completed poem and feeling our forehead and shirt soaked with sweat.

Not knowing what the depth or absence of your interest in literature is, Isaac, we are sending along just the two poems, set out below, and if you convey to us that you have interest in seeing the entire collection of poems, we will gladly send you the same. Although a few might notice that the first poem follows the look and patterns of traditional verse, presenting, as it does, two sonnets. Of course, it may be safely assumed that the Spectral Handler, all-knowing as He is, is well schooled in classical verse, yet He also entertains experimentation in art as well, as is shown in the deviations He played at in the composition of the second poem sent herewith, which were no doubt entirely deliberate.

A Would-be Moses

1.
In G-d's eyes, a flame flashed a blade
When I raised my eyes to His—blue-
Orange fire, razor sharp, drew my blood
To the surface: "I want to talk to you,"
I said, "that's all." "Alright, but you remind
Me of another who required plagues and
Parting a sea. Even if you're more refined,
You've also needs and the wounded land,
Bruised black, gashed with wind, speaks
To you, as if the soil were your own skin."
G-d smiled, knowing what each man seeks,

That I'd nothing new, yet he continued, "Begin
Mortal man, what would you ask of Me,
You, who sin and have eyes but do not see?"

2.
"Of course, You are right, but teach me to see then,
Dear G-d, leave me less inclined to sin, and rage not
At the land, but me, if it is I who sin again and again?
Help me untangle the knot of Self, learn all we forgot
Since we were first exiled from the Garden and give
Me just a glimpse, at least, of the ineffable—to see You
So I might, in my small way, be able to help others live
As you would have us." "What you ask, if made true,
Amounts to as much or more than parting any sea.
The glimpse you ask for is bold too—need I remind
You, even Moses, beloved by Me, could only see
Me, though ready for a fearful end, from behind!"
"Fine, then free me from this mortal cage—
Man fails, so punish me to end Your rage!"

The Temple under a Red Sky

Before You, King of kings, I bend my knee and bow.
Having risen from my bed just now,
still shaking the vision in my head,
I know You, the Holy One, understand:

I was inside the shadowy, white stone Temple, tall,
its archways and walls towering beyond my feelings,
though hanging firmly from gold leaf ceilings, some
lines in Hebrew, I couldn't read, were on the wall,
but sensed it suggested something about Home,
where my journey would end and I'd not be alone.

But then, shuffling to me, I saw many creatures:
cyclopes possessing malformed heads lacking hair,

then drunken wizened men whose twisting torsos
ended in one leg, while others with crescent beaks
for mouths chattered in a high pitched, clicking tongue.
A language of their own—nonsense that hung in the air.

I ran outside of the Temple to escape these creatures,
chased by bleak fears and the chill of ancient prophecies,
but then, in my linen tunic, fell on my back staring at a sky
that resembled Hell, aflame in brilliant red with waves
and bursts of fire, the color of blood. Finally, I cried
out to You, Creator of all, and then the cackling creatures,

the crackling flames above—all dissipated, all was silence.
Then, You, dear G-d, declared: "Now see the divine you sought."
So, I opened my eyes: Blue was the sky, the sun yellow, new—
though the Temple was in ruins, it was cleansed of demons.
"You lay Abram, but arise now, Magnus Pater," You, my G-d,
instructed me, "bring others unto you to celebrate My love."